이베리아의 전갈

〈K-픽션〉 시리즈는 한국문학의 젊은 상상력입니다. 최근 발표된 가장 우수하고 흥미로운 작품을 엄선하여 출간하는 〈K-픽션〉은 한국문학의 생생한 현장을 국내외 독자들과 실시간으로 공유하고자 기획되었습니다. 〈바이링궐 에디션 한국 대표 소설〉 시리즈를 통해 검증된 탁월한 번역진이 참여하여 원작의 재미와 품격을 최대한 살린 〈K-픽션〉 시리즈는 매 계절마다 새로운 작품을 선보입니다.

This 〈K-Fiction〉 Series represents the brightest of young imaginative voices in contemporary Korean fiction. Each issue consists of a wide range of outstanding contemporary Korean short stories that the editorial board of *Asia* carefully selects each season. These stories are then translated by professional Korean literature translators, all of whom take special care to faithfully convey the pieces' original tones and grace. We hope that, each and every season, these exceptional young Korean voices will delight and challenge all of you, our treasured readers both here and abroad.

이베리아의 전갈
Dishonored

최민우 | 전승희 옮김
Written by Choi Min-woo
Translated by Jeon Seung-hee

ASIA
PUBLISHERS

Contents

이베리아의 전갈
Dishonored

블랙은 분수쇼의 순서라면 훤히 꿰고 있었다.

왈츠에 맞춰 물줄기들이 솟아올랐다. 복합쇼핑몰과 비즈니스호텔 사이의 공터에 조성된 인공연못의 바닥에서 조명이 알록달록하게 반짝였다.

블랙은 쇼핑몰 난간에 기대어 쇼를 지켜봤다. 솟아오르다 떨어지는 물을 따라 고개를 올리고 숙였다. 옐로는 연못 앞 벤치에 앉아 있었다. 용이 승천하듯 날아오른 굵은 물줄기 세 개가 쇼핑몰 옥상과 호텔의 발코니를 연결한 붉은 천을 사정없이 두드렸다. 폭죽들이 팡팡 터지자 불꽃들이 환하게 피어올랐다. 쇼를 구경하던 사람들이 박수를 쳤다. 옐로도 그들과 함께 손을 팔랑

Black was on top of the water fountain show sequence.

Streams of water soared along to a waltz. Colorful lights shimmered at the bottom of the artificial pond in the empty lot between the shopping mall and the business hotel.

Black watched the show, leaning against the railings of the mall. His face went up and down, following the water's soaring and falling movements. Yellow was sitting on a bench in front of the pond. Three thick streams soared dragon-like and battered the red cloth hanging between the shopping mall rooftop and the hotel balcony. Firecrackers exploded and flowers made of flames bloomed

거렸다.

쇼가 끝나고 가로등에 설치된 스피커에서 달콤한 라운지 음악이 흘러나왔다. 옐로가 자리를 털고 일어났다. 블랙은 거리를 두고 그를 따라갔다. 호텔 앞 버스정류장에서 서성이던 옐로는 잠시 뒤 도착한 노란색 버스에 올라탔다. 블랙은 그가 어디서 내릴지, 내린 다음 어디로 갈지, 밤에는 무엇을 할지 모두 알고 있었다. 그런 건 문제가 아니었다.

진짜 문제는 더 이상 그걸 알아야 하는지 확실치 않다는 데 있었다.

모두들 옐로가 명예롭게 은퇴할 자격이 충분하다고 생각했다. 그는 평생 회사에 헌신했고 현장에서 몇 번의 중요한 작전을 성공적으로 이끌었다. 그중 하나로 비공식적인 장관 표창을 받기도 했다. 일선에서 사무실로 자리를 옮긴 뒤에는 복잡하게 엉킨 서류를 정리하고 부서 간의 이해관계를 조정하며 세월을 보냈다. 부인과는 사별했으며 딸은 스위스 남자와 결혼해 뉴질랜드에서 살았는데, 부녀 사이는 좋지 않은 걸로 알려졌다. 사내에서는 무던한 상관이자 큰 야심은 없는 부하로 평가

brilliantly. The spectators clapped. Yellow flapped his hands together along with them.

After the show was over, sweet, mellow music from the hotel lounge flowed out of speakers attached to streetlights. Yellow got up. Black left his post to follow after him. Yellow hesitated for a moment at the bus stop in front of the hotel, but got on the yellow bus that arrived soon afterwards. Black knew which stop he would get off at, where he would head after that, and what he would do at night. But none of that really mattered.

What really mattered to him at the moment was that he did not know whether or not he should keep on knowing Yellow's schedule.

Everyone thought Yellow deserved to retire honorably. He had dedicated his entire life to his company and successfully led a few major operations during his fieldwork. He had even won an unofficial award from the ministry for a certain successful operation. After he was transferred to the office, he had spent his time putting complicated data in order and ironing out the differences of opinions among a number of different departments. His wife died and he had a daughter who married a Swiss man and lived in New Zealand. It was known that

받았다.

관례대로라면 해외 지부 부임은 공직생활을 마감하는 포상이어야 했다. 출장 오는 외교부 관리들과 갈 만한 온천을 확보하고 대사관 리셉션에서 연어샐러드를 집어먹는 게 업무의 전부여야 했다. 그렇게 쉬다 귀국하면 적당한 수준의 노후대책이 회사 마크가 찍힌 금시계와 함께 깔끔하게 포장되어 그를 기다릴 것이었다. 연금이 모자라다 싶으면 택시 운전대라도 잡고 소일하면 될 일이었다.

피곤한 마무리는 아무도 원하지 않았다.

시작은 돌이켜보면 어이없을 정도로 사소했다. 신임 지부장을 환영하는 만찬이 열렸고, 기분 좋게 취한 사람들이 민들레 홀씨처럼 만찬장을 여유롭게 돌아다녔다. 전임 지부장과 옐로도 서로의 업적을 칭찬하며 즐거운 시간을 보냈다. 그러다 칭찬할 업적이 떨어졌을 때쯤 전임 지부장이 옐로가 받은 표창에 대해 가벼운 농담을 던졌는데, 옐로는 그 농담을 당시 작전에 문제가 있었다는 뜻으로 받아들였다. 말하기 좋아하는 사람들은 그때 전임 지부장이 제대로 사과를 해야 했다고 떠들어댔지만 그가 사과를 할 줄 아는 사람이었다면 그

he and his daughter were not on good terms. In his company, he was considered a generous superior and a not so ambitious subordinate.

According to custom, his transfer to an overseas post should have meant a final reward to his lengthy official career. His entire work duties at his new post should have involved nothing more than securing spas to take diplomats on their business trips and eating salmon salad in embassy receptions. When he returned home after enjoying this sort of vacation, he should have been met with a decent level retirement package, tidily wrapped together with a gold watch, the company logo engraved on it. If his pension wasn't enough, he could while away his time driving a taxi.

Nobody wanted to finish tired.

In retrospect, the beginning of this whole affair had been absurdly trivial. As a newly appointed branch chief, he had been welcomed with a reception where happily and moderately drunk people milled around the hall leisurely like dandelion pollens adrift. At first, Yellow's predecessor and Yellow had had a nice time, taking turns praising each other's respective achievements. When they were left with no more items left to laud each other for, Yellow's predecessor had lightly joked about Yel-

자리까지 올라가기나 했을까? 인수인계 과정에서 자잘한 의견 충돌이 겹치면서 분위기가 점점 험악해졌고, 급기야 옐로는 전임 지부장이 공금을 횡령했다고 회사에 보고하기에 이르렀다. 다시 한번, 말하기 좋아하는 사람들은 회사가 좋은 게 좋은 거라는 식으로 적당히 넘어가면 안 되는 거였다고 재잘거렸지만 은퇴가 눈앞인 고위 공무원에게 얼마나 엄격한 잣대를 들이댈 수 있었을까? 회사는 적절한 조치를 취하겠다고 답변해놓고서는 옐로가 감찰기관에 독단으로 감사를 청구할 때까지 그 건에 대해 까맣게 잊고 있었다. 일이 터지고 나서야 회사는 옐로에게 청구를 철회할지 품위유지 규정위반으로 정직 처분을 받아 연금을 날릴지 둘 중 하나를 고르라고 엄격하게 요구했다. 옐로는 세 번째, 그러니까 언론에 이 사실을 폭로하는 길을 선택했고, 내친김에 지부의 다른 부패까지 다 터뜨렸다. 문제가 커지자 회사는 옐로를 강제 귀국시키려고 했지만 그는 범죄인 인도협정이 체결되지 않은 나라로 몸을 피했다.

"그래 놓고선 책을 쓴대."

국장이 블랙을 따로 호출해서 말했다.

"그쪽에 있는 우리 참사관이 설득하러 갔는데 팔을

low's award. Yellow took it as a veiled criticism about that particular operation he had carried out. Meddlesome people later said that the predecessor should have apologized on the spot, but if the predecessor had been someone who knew how to apologize, would he have ever risen to the position he had?

A few more trivial conflicts during the transition made things worse, and in the end, Yellow reported to company heads that his predecessor had embezzled company money. Again, meddlesome third parties claimed that the company shouldn't simply have attempted to cover all of this up – how could the company have treated someone on the verge of retirement this severely? The company replied that they would take appropriate measures and then completely forgot until Yellow independently requested inspection from the inspection office. Only after this did the company present its ultimatum: choose between withdrawing the request or suffer suspension from office without pension. By making an inspection request, Yellow would have denigrated his own office. Yellow chose neither. Instead, he took the matter to the media. While doing this, he disclosed various other forms of corruption in the company as well. When

뒤로 쫙 비틀면서 그러더래. 책. 웹사이트 이딴 것도 아
니고, 책. 뭐 어쩌라는 건지 모르겠어. 예전 작전들을 몽
땅 불 생각인가 봐. 미친 거지. 기밀 해제가 안 된 게 거
의 다야. 이 엄중한 시국에! 이 새끼는……."

국장이 입버릇인 '엄중한 시국'을 들먹이며 욕을 퍼붓
기 시작했다. 블랙은 책상 위에 진열된 각종 감사패에
시선을 둔 채 상관의 분노가 가라앉길 기다렸다. 국장
은 전날 비공개로 진행됐던 회의에서 골프채를 휘두르
며 공포 분위기를 조성했다. 다들 레고 블록처럼 허리
를 뻣뻣이 세운 채 앉아 있어야 했다.

숨을 돌린 국장이 전자담배 버튼을 누르고 한 모금
빨았다.

"일단 목표는 귀국을 시키는 거야. 그런데 반드시 귀
국을 시킬 필요는 없어. 현장에는 변수가 많잖아. 반항
할 수도 있고, 또 뭐냐…… 강하게 반항할 수도 있지.
현장에서 독자적으로 잘 판단을 내리면 돼. 데리고 올
수 있느냐, 없느냐, 없다면 어떻게 하느냐, 그런 판단들.
무슨 말인지 알지?"

블랙은 그 말의 속뜻을 곱씹었다.

"알겠습니다."

things were getting out of hand, the company tried to force him to return home, but he escaped to another country that had no extradition treaty with his own.

"Now, I hear he's writing a book," the bureau director told Black. Black had just arrived, at request of the director's summons.

"He just put his arms behind him and told our embassy councilor he would when he went to persuade him. A book, not just a website, but a book. I'm not sure what he wants. Looks like he is planning on revealing all our past operations. Crazy! Almost all of them are still classified. And in this grave situation! That son-of-a-bitch..."

The bureau director brought up "this grave situation" as usual and began cursing. Black waited for his superior's rage to subside, letting his gaze travel from commendation plaque to commendation plaque displayed all across the director's desk. The bureau director had brandished a golf club at all attendees during the closed-door meeting the previous day. All of them had had to sit straight in their seats like Lego blocks.

After pausing a moment to take a breath, the bureau director pressed the button on his E-cigarette and breathed in.

"질문 있나?"

"지부장이 말년에 갑자기 왜 폭주하는지 혹시 짐작 가는 바라도?"

"내가 어제 너희들한테 물어본 게 그거잖아. 근데 아무도 대답을 안 했지? 내 생각엔 같은 밥만 수십 년을 먹어서 돌아버린 것 같애. 구내식당 밥이 좀 그렇잖아. 그리고 그 인간 지부장이라 부르지 마. 듣는 국장 기분 나빠."

구내식당 밥은 먹지도 않는 국장이 지쳤다는 듯 의자에 몸을 파묻으며 눈을 감았다.

공항에 밴을 몰고 블랙을 마중나온 사람은 브라운이라는 해외 주재원이었다. 얇은 청록색 니트에 감색 바지를 입고 있었는데, 시내까지 가는 내내 틈만 나면 옷에 달린 보풀을 뜯어댔고 블랙과 통 눈을 마주치려 들지 않았다. 그러면서도 입은 쉴 줄을 몰랐다. 블랙에 대해 많이 들었다면서 늘 존경해 왔다는 입에 발린 말을 되풀이했다. 카오디오에서는 소닉유스의 로큰롤이 징징거렸고, 블랙은 음악 소리 때문에 신경을 바짝 곤두세운 채 브라운이 작성한 보고서를 글로브박스에서 꺼

"Our primary directive is to bring him back home. But, at the same time, we don't necessarily have to have him here. There are many variables in the field, aren't there? He might resist, and ... He might resort to force, you see? You can make the appropriate decision independently on the spot. Take him home or don't take him home. If you don't believe it's possible to bring him back, take necessary measures, whatever you see fit. Understood?"

Black thought it over.

"Yes, sir!"

"Any questions?"

"Do you have any idea why the branch chief would suddenly go out of his mind at the end of his career?"

"I asked you the same thing yesterday. But nobody answered, did they? I guess he went nuts after eating the same food every day for a few decades. You know the cafeteria food is pretty ridiculous. By the way, don't call that S.O.B. the "branch chief." It makes me sick."

The bureau director, who did not eat the cafeteria food himself, sat back deeply into his chair and closed his eyes, as if he was exhausted.

A branch officer named Brown came to pick up

내 읽었다.

　보고서에 따르면 옐로는 잔디처럼 단조로운 일상을 보내는 중이었다. 그는 시내 중심가의 오피스텔에 방을 얻어 살았다. 새벽에 일어나 강변을 산책한 다음 오전 내내 시립도서관에서 신문을 탐독했다. 가끔 뭔가를 복사하거나 출력해서 들고 나오기도 했다. 오후에는 커피숍에서 카페 주인이 기르는 삼색털 고양이와 노닥거리거나 집에서 TV를 봤고 저녁에는 때때로 근처 쇼핑몰로 버스를 타고 가 지역 명물인 분수쇼를 구경했다. 브라운은 오피스텔 건물 앞에서 옐로에게 팔이 비틀린 참사관이 그물에 걸린 고기마냥 파닥거리며 발을 구르는 걸 봤지만 개입하지 말라는 지시를 받았기 때문에 보기만 했다고 설명했다.

　"영감 정정하던데요."

　"그럴 거야."

　블랙이 대답했다. 입사 초기에 블랙은 옐로의 팀에서 일한 적이 있었다. 당시 옐로는 현장에서 관리직으로 막 발령을 받은 참이었고, 거리의 먼지와 손끝에서 뚝뚝 듣는 고문실의 비명, 그리고 강철 같은 호승심을 완전히 씻어내지 못한 상태였다. 블랙은 그와 스쿼시를

Black on a van to the airport. He was wearing a thin bluish green knit shirt and navy blue pants. Brown kept picking at his shirt, which had begun to bunch in certain places, and then tried to avoid making eye contact with Black. Still, Brown's mouth didn't stop moving, saying that he'd heard a lot about Black and that he'd long admired him. He repeated this lip service over and over. Sonic Youth was blaring out of the car stereo. Black took out a report Brown had prepared from the glove compartment and read it, his nerves on edge because of the music.

According to the report, Yellow was living a life as monotonous as the life of a well-trimmed lawn. He lived in a downtown office studio. He woke up early in the morning, took walks along the river, and then methodically digested a newspaper in the city library for the rest of the morning. Occasionally he copied or printed something and brought this with him from the library. In the afternoon, he hung out at a café, usually playing with the owner's tri-colored cat while there, or he watched TV at home. In the evening, he sometimes took a bus to a nearby shopping mall and watched the water fountain show, one of the local attractions. Brown said that although he'd seen Yellow and the embassy coun-

같이 쳤다가 까무러칠 뻔했던 기억이 지금도 생생했다. 그는 성공적인 적응을 위해 포르티시모밖에 모르는 피아니스트처럼 컴퓨터 자판을 두드리고 엑셀과 파워포인트를 IED 제조법처럼 공부했었다.

"그분 메이저는 뭐였더랍니까? 혹시 아세요? 선배라고 불러도 되지요?"

시내로 진입하는 인터체인지에서 차가 밀리는 동안 브라운이 말했다.

"파괴공작. 좋도록 해."

"알겠습니다, 선배. 뭘 파괴했는데요?"

"부술 수 있는 조직은 몽땅."

"이젠 자기가 파괴당할 차례인 거네요."

브라운이 신경질적으로 웃었다. 블랙은 그 웃음소리를 듣자 좀 걱정이 됐다. 결정적인 순간에 헛손질을 하면 곤란했다.

그날 저녁 그들은 브라운이 은신처로 임대한 작은 맨션에서 종이그릇에 포장해 온 중국 음식을 먹었다. 브라운은 혼자 파견된 해외 주재원들이 종종 그렇듯 향수병과 스트레스에 시달리고 있었다. 곁에 사람이 생기자 응석을 부렸고 맥주 한 잔에 얼굴이 빨개지더니 고향에

cilor together once—the councilor's arms were bent back and twisted by Yellow, the councilor wriggling like a fish caught in a net—, Brown had just watched. He'd been ordered to avoid direct contact with Yellow.

"That old man's still hale and hearty."

"He must be," Black said.

When Black was a newcomer, he had worked in Yellow's team for a while. Having just been transferred from the field to an office post, Yellow still hadn't completely shaken off the street dust, the torture room screams that seemed to come from his fingertips, and a steel-like competitive spirit inside him. Black still remembered vividly that he'd almost fainted playing squash with him. In order to adapt to his office post successfully, Yellow had tapped the computer keyboard like a pianist who only knew fortissimo and had learned Excel and PowerPoint like he was learning how to make an IED.

"What was his major? Do you know by any chance? May I call you *seonbae*[1]?" Brown asked Black, when they were stuck in a traffic jam at the traffic circle by the downtown street entrance.

1) *Seonbae* is a name for one's old alum, usually at school, but often in other places including one's workplace.

있는 딸 사진도 보여줬다. 버섯 모양의 커다란 느티나
무를 배경으로 아빠와는 전혀 닮지 않은 통통한 여자애
가 아들을 빼다 박은 할머니 옆에서 심통 어린 표정으
로 서 있었다.

두 잔째에는 급격히 우울해지면서 칭얼거렸다.

"제가 잘할 수 있을까요?"

"종교랑 똑같은 거다. 세상 사람들이 아무리 뭐라 그
래도 나는 떳떳해야 돼. 그게 안 될 거 같으면 지금 짐
싸서 돌아가."

"종교." 브라운이 입맛을 다셨다. "뭘 믿는 종교입니
까?"

"뭘 믿느냐가 중요한 게 아냐. 믿는 게 중요한 거지.
뭐든 믿어. 나라. 민족. 이념. 가족. 돈. 나 자신. 하다못
해 하느님이라도. 많잖아. 그걸 위해서 일한다고 생각
하라고."

"연수원에서는 국가에 충성하라고 그러던데요."

"처음엔 그걸로 시작해도 괜찮고."

"그럼 전 가족을 믿겠습니다." 브라운이 젓가락으로
그릇 안에 든 볶음 면을 휘저었다. "선배는 뭘 믿습니
까? 물어봐도 됩니까?"

"Destruction operation. Do as you please."

"Ok, *seonbae*. What did he destroy?"

"Whatever organization that needed to be destroyed—all of them."

"And now it's his turn, then."

Brown laughed nervously. That laughter worried Black a little. It would not do if he made a mistake at a critical moment.

That evening, they ate Chinese food from paper containers in a small apartment Brown had rented as his hideout. Brown was struggling with homesickness and stress, as most overseas agents dispatched alone were. Happy to have a guest, he was playing the baby. His face flushed after only one glass of beer. He showed Black his daughter's picture at home. There was a large zelkova tree in the shape of a mushroom that stood as the backdrop. A chubby girl who did not resemble her father at all stood sullenly next to her grandmother who looked exactly like her father.

After two glasses of beer, Brown quickly became gloomy and peevish.

"Do you think I can do this?" Brown asked.

"It's like religion. Whatever other people in the world say, I should feel honorable. If you don't think you can do that, then just pack up and go

"나는……" 블랙이 말했다. "이게 내 일이라는 걸 믿지."

세 잔째가 되자 브라운은 기분이 좋아졌다.

"이런 일 자주 하세요? 사람 많이 죽여보셨어요? 형님이라 불러도 되죠? 저 형님이 왜 이리 맘에 드나 모르겠습니다."

"누구 맘대로 형님이래."

"이런 일 말입니다, 몇 번 하면 익숙해지나요?"

"계속 싼다고 변비가 익숙해지는 거 봤냐."

브라운이 다시 신경질적으로 웃었다.

"그거 좀 재미없네요, 형님."

다음날 블랙은 옐로와 함께 강변에 나갔다. 보고서에 첨부된 사진으로 확인하긴 했지만 막상 망원렌즈를 통해 산책 중인 옐로를 실제로 보자 블랙은 조금 충격을 받았다. 샛노랗게 떨어지는 아침 햇살이 찰랑이는 물결 위에서 바스라지고 공기 속 희미한 열기가 더운 하루를 예고하는 가운데, 초라한 매무새의 가무잡잡한 노인이 우레탄 재질로 된 벽돌색 산책로 위를 구부정한 자세로 걷고 있었다. 자전거를 탄 날렵한 남자들과 고무공처럼 통통 튀며 조깅을 하는 날씬한 여자들 사이에서 그는

home right now."

"Religion," Brown smacked his lips. "What am I supposed to believe?"

"What you believe in doesn't matter. It's the believing that matters. Believe in whatever—your country, your nation, ideology, family, money, yourself... at least, God. There are so many things to believe in. Whatever it is, think that you work for that."

"At the training institute, they told us to be loyal to our state."

"You can start with that."

"Then, I'll believe in my family."

Brown stirred the fried noodles in his bowl with his chopsticks.

"What do you believe in, *seonbae*? May I ask you?"

"I..." Black said, "I believe that this is my job."

After the third glass, Brown finally relaxed.

"Do you do this kind of work often? Have you killed many people? May I call you *hyeongnim*[2]? I don't know why I like you, *hyeongnim*, so much."

"Who told you that you could call me *hyeongnim*?"

"This kind of job, y'know. Do you get used to it after a few go-rounds?"

---

2) *Hyeongnim* is originally a respectful name for one's elder brother, but it is often used for strangers older than oneself whom one feels close to.

마치 다른 시공간의 물결을 거슬러올라가는 사람마냥 꾸물대다가 슬며시 산책로를 벗어났다. 그리고는 잔디에 앉아 울적한 표정으로 텀블러에 든 음료수를 빨대로 마시며 강물을 바라보았다.

"저럴 때 보면 알아서 죽어줄 것 같은데 말이지요……."

브라운이 말했다.

블랙은 옐로의 동선을 조그만 화이트보드 위에 그렸다. 그는 해가 떴을 때 사방이 트인 장소만을 다녔고 밤에도 조명이 환한 곳만 찾았다. 음식점이나 카페에서는 출입구가 잘 보이는 자리에 벽을 등지고 앉았다. 경찰이나 경비원의 도움을 언제든 요청할 수 있도록 호루라기를 목에 걸고 다녔다. 배달 식료품이나 세탁물은 오피스텔 입구 경비실에 놓아두도록 한 다음 경비원이 보는 앞에서 찾아갔다.

그들은 몇 가지 계획을 세웠지만 모두 만족스럽지 않았다. 무엇보다 현지 사법당국, 특히 오피스텔에서 한 블록 떨어진 곳에 위치한 경찰서와 마찰을 일으키는 일을 피해야 했는데 그러기가 쉽지 않았다. 결국 새벽에 화재경보기를 오작동시켜 놀란 사람들이 밖으로 나왔

"Do you get used to constipation if you keep having it?"

Brown laughed again, nervously.

"That's no fun, *hyeongnim*."

The next day, Black went out to the riverbank to shadow Yellow. Although he had already seen his picture attached to the report, Black was still a little shocked to see Yellow through a telephoto lens. As the bright yellow morning sunrays broke into pieces over the lapping waves and the faint heat in the air predicted a hot day, a shabbily clad, tanned old man, his body slight and bent, walked along a brick-colored, polyurethane path. Amidst trim male cyclists and female joggers bouncing along the path like rubber balls, he moved slowly, like someone going against the current of a different time and place. He left the walking path. Then he sat down on the lawn and looked down at the river. He drank moodily from his tumbler straw.

"Moments like these, he looks like he's about to die from natural causes..." Brown said.

Black traced Yellow's movements on a small white board. He went only to open places while the sun was out, and looked for only brightly lit places at night. When he was in restaurant or café, he sat at a seat near the entrance with his back

을 때 브라운이 준비해 둔 다른 은신처로 데려가 마무리를 짓는다는 그림을 그렸다. 실행은 이틀 뒤 새벽으로 잡았다.

"선배, 돌아갈 때 이거 애 선물로 괜찮을까요?"

면세점 사이트에 뜬 인형 사진을 보여주며 브라운이 말했다.

다음 날, 블랙의 고국에서 쿠데타가 발발했다.

블랙은 계속 TV 뉴스를 켜두고 틈나는 대로 인터넷 브라우저의 새로고침 아이콘을 눌렀다. 정확히 무슨 일이 벌어지고 있는지 아무도 몰랐다. 어순과 단어만 다르게 배치한 헤드라인이 TV 화면 아래를 계속 지나갔다. 앵커는 쿠데타군이 제공한 영상을 반복해서 내보내며 새로운 소식이 들어오는 대로 보도하겠다는 말만 되풀이했다. 블랙은 꿈에서도 그 영상을 볼 정도였다. 수도의 광장에 사람들이 모여 있었다. 그들을 가로막듯 늘어선 탱크와 군용지프의 벽 뒤에서 선글라스를 쓰고 목에 쌍안경을 건 군복 차림의 키 크고 여윈 남자가 나타났다. 남자는 사람들 앞으로 당당히 혼자 나아갔다. 블랙은 화면 밖에 배치된 저격수들과 경호원들이 눈에

against the wall. He carried a whistle around his neck so that he could ask for help from policemen or guards as soon as he needed. He had his groceries and laundries delivered to the guard's room at the entrance of his office studio building and claimed them right in front of the guard.

They tried to come up with a few plans, but they were all unsatisfactory. Above all, they had to avoid a clash with the judicial system of the country, especially the police only a block away from the office studio. This, however, turned out to be a difficult task. In the end, they settled on a plan to set off the fire alarm, grab Yellow when he exited the building, take him to another hideout that they already had ready, and then finish him off there. They planned to do all of this in two days.

"*Seonbae*, what do you think of this as a gift for my daughter?" Brown said, pointing to at a photo of a doll on a duty-free shop website.

The next day, a coup d'état occurred in Black's home country.

Black left his TV on and he would press the reset icon on his Internet browser from time to time. Nobody knew exactly what was happening. Headlines with the same words arranged differently, or

선했다. 광장의 사람들이 팔을 추켜올리고 박수를 치고 국기를 흔들었다. 블랙은 그 선글라스 낀 군인을 요주의 인물만 따로 모아놓은 스크랩에서 본 기억이 있었다. 그 사진에선 선글라스를 끼고 있지 않아서 알아보는 데 시간이 걸리긴 했다. 아무튼 지금으로서는 그 영상만이 블랙이 알던 세상이 바뀌었다는 증거였다. 깨진 유리창도, 우왕좌왕하는 사람들도, 엉망진창이 된 거리도 보이지 않았다. 당연했다. 정보 통제는 기본 중의 기본이었다. 누군지는 모르겠지만 일 하나는 제대로 하고 있었다.

쿠데타군과 정부군 사이에 교전이 벌어졌다는 루머가 트위터와 페이스북을 통해 전파되었다. 다수의 사상자가 발생했다는 소리도 있었고 민간인 피해가 상상 이상으로 심각하다는 말도 있었지만 확인할 길이 없었다. 계엄상황에서 '일시적 전산상의 오류'가 일어나 인터넷이 차단됐기 때문이었다.

"해저 케이블을 아예 끊어버린 건지도 몰라요. 정말 그러면 미친 건데."

브라운이 식은땀을 흘리며 말했다. 그는 정신없이 노트북을 두드리며 본국 인터넷에 접속할 수 있는 우회

replaced with other words with the same meanings, kept passing by at the bottom of the screen. The anchorman kept showing the same images the coup d'état forces offered, saying he would report the news as soon as new information was available. Black would see the same images even in his dreams. There were crowds in the capital's central square. A tall, thin man in a military uniform wearing sunglasses and binoculars around his neck appeared behind rows of tanks and military jeeps, standing in front of the crowds as if to block them. The man walked forward, alone and majestically. Black could picture the snipers and bodyguards stationed outside the screen vividly. The crowds in the square raised their arms, cheering and waving national flags. Black remembered seeing the picture of the soldier wearing sunglasses in a scrapbook, a collection of people who had been under surveillance. He wasn't wearing sunglasses in this picture, though, so it took Black some time to recognize him. At any rate, at the moment, those images were the only evidence that proved the world Black had known had changed. He could not see any broken glasses, people in their confusion, or damaged streets. Information control was a basic requirement in a situation like this. Whoever the

가능한 서버를 필사적으로 찾아다녔다. 교전이 벌어졌다고 추정되는 곳은 브라운의 고향이었다.

블랙은 대사관에 가 사정을 알아보려 했지만 그쪽도 넋이 나가 뒤숭숭하긴 마찬가지였다. 휴교령이 내린 학교에 간 기분이었다. 겨우 만난 참사관은 동요하지 말고 평소처럼 각자의 자리에서 맡은 바 임무를 다 하라는 메시지를 받은 게 전부라고 블랙에게 말했다.

"근데 그게 어느 쪽에서 온 메시지인지 알 수가 없더란 말이지."

참사관이 여전히 불편한 오른쪽 어깨를 주무르며 입맛을 다셨다.

"임무는 어떻게 되는 겁니까?"

브라운이 말했다. 눈가는 까맣게 가라앉았고 입술에 물집이 돋아 있었다.

"지시가 있을 때까진 대기한다."

"현장 판단이 중요하다고 국장님이 그러지 않았습니까."

블랙이 브라운의 얼굴을 후려쳤다.

"이게 현장 판단이다. 정신 바짝 차려. 지금 정신줄 놓으면 죽도 밥도 안 돼."

man was, he knew how to handle the situation.

A rumor that there was open combat between the coup d'état forces and the governmental forces was circulating on Twitter and Facebook. Some reported that many people had been killed or injured. Others said that the number of civilian casualties was unimaginable—but there was no way to confirm this news. The Internet was blocked due to a "temporary electrical failure" under the country's martial law.

"They might have just cut the underwater cables. If they did that, though, that's absurd." Brown said, breaking out in a cold sweat. He was tapping away at his laptop keyboard frantically, trying to find a server that could reroute and connect him to the Internet of his home country. The area where people were conjecturing combat was already taking place was his own hometown.

Black went to the embassy to find out what happened, but all he found was chaos. No one knew what had happened or what to do. The embassy was like a school ordered temporarily closed. When the embassy councilor managed to finally meet with Black he merely informed him that his only message ordered its readers to stay calm and to continue their work as if nothing had happened.

브라운이 블랙을 노려보았다.

"알겠습니다. 선배님은 일을 믿지요. 저는 인간을 믿어서 그렇게 냉정하질 못하겠네요."

다음 날 아침 브라운은 사라졌다. 그들이 계획했던 내용이 적힌 화이트보드와 옐로의 오피스텔 청사진, 방 평면도, 배선 관련 장비 몇 가지가 책상 위에 가지런히 정리된 채 놓여 있었다. 청사진에 붙어 있는 건 화재경보기 조작법에 대한 알기 쉽고 자세한 설명이 적힌 노란 포스트잇이었다. 그래도 정신줄은 놓지 않았다는 무언의 항변이 빈 방을 뱅글뱅글 돌고 있었다.

국장과 전화 연결이 되었을 때 블랙은 하마터면 소리를 빽 하고 지를 뻔했다.

"상황이 좋지 않아. 그러니까……"

"엄중한 시국인 거죠."

"그렇지. 엄중한 시국."

국장이 말했다. 통화 상태가 나빠 말이 띄엄띄엄 이어졌다.

"다 엉망이야. 사방이 적이라고. 교전? 국지성 충돌이 있었던 건 맞아. 정확한 피해는 아직 집계되지 않았고. 분명한 게 없어……"

"But I have no idea which side sent that message to us," the councilor said, smacking his lips while massaging his own uncomfortable right shoulder.

"What should I do about my work?" Brown said. His eyes were deeply sunken and there were blisters around his lips.

"We should stand by until a further order comes."

"Didn't the director say that on-the-spot decision-making was important?"

Black slapped Brown in the face.

"Here's an on-the-spot decision. Stay alert. If you don't, you'll lose everything."

Brown glared at Black.

"I got it. You, *seonbae*, believe in the work. But I believe in people, so I can't just stay so calm."

The next morning, Brown disappeared. In their room there was nothing left but a white board with their plans posted on it, a blueprint of Yellow's building, the ground plans of Yellow's unit, and a few wiring tools tidily arranged on the desk. A yellow post-it with easy, detailed instructions on how to operate the fire alarm was attached to the blueprint. Brown's silent protest that he did stay alert seemed to haunt the empty room.

When he finally managed to connect to the director by phone, Black almost found himself

블랙은 기가 찼다. 어떻게 회사가 이걸 모를 수 있단 말인가? 어떤 사전징후도 없었나? 보고체계는 어찌된 건가? 정기적으로 받는 정보보고만 주의깊게 검토했어도 알 수 있는 일 아니었나? 이렇게 무력하게 당한다는 게 말이 되나?

"임무는 어떻게 되는 겁니까?"

"임무? 그렇지. 임무가 있었지."

국장의 목소리가 수평선 너머의 뱃고동처럼 희미하게 울렸다.

"임무에는 변동사항이 없어. 목표를 시야에서 놓치지 말고 대기하도록 해. 임무를 속행할 때가 되면 알려줄……"

전화가 끊겼다. 블랙은 전화기를 손에 들고 침대에 걸터앉았다. 어딘가의 통신센터가 파괴된 모양이었다.

아니면 통화 자체가 꿈이었을지도 몰랐다.

쿠데타 소식은 뉴스 상단에서 하단으로 미끄러져 내려갔다. 다른 나라에서 벌어진, 국내 정세에 영향을 미치지 않는 정변에 계속 신경을 쓰기에는 더 중요한 일들이 많았다. 물가가 계속 올랐다. 제조업의 둔화가 뚜

shouting.

"The situation is not—optimal..." the director trailed off.

"I see. It's quite grave, isn't it?" Black said.

"That's right. Quite grave."

The phone connection was fairly poor, so their conversation progressed haltingly.

"Everything's a mess. Enemies are surrounding us. Combat? It's true that there were local confrontations. The exact number of casualties isn't yet clear. Nothing's clear..."

Black was dumbfounded. How could the company not have known all of this? Had there been no hint of this happening? What about the report structure? Couldn't they have predicted this just by carefully examining periodic intelligence reports? How could the company be so helpless?

"What about my mission, sir?"

"Mission? Oh. That."

The director's voice was as faint as a boat whistle beyond the horizon.

"There's no change in your mission. Don't lose your target and stand by. I'll let you know when to resume..."

The phone disconnected. Black sat on the edge of his bed with the receiver in his hand. A commu-

39

렷해졌다. 시골 마을에서 머리 없는 시체가 발견되었다. 유명 여배우가 시사회장에서 노브라로 레드카펫을 밟았다. 아프리카에서는 아이들이 굶어 죽어갔다.

세상의 관심이 줄어들수록 정보는 늘어났다. 쿠데타 정부는 비상위원회를 설치한 뒤 구태와 부패의 청산을 제일의 목표로 삼아 혁명적 개혁을 통해 내부의 적을 축출하고 외부의 위협에 맞서 민주적 체제를 유지하겠다는 로드맵을 공표했다. 공해상을 벗어난 비행기가 급작스런 기류 변화로 추락했는데, 거기에 전 정부의 주요 인사들이 타고 있었다는 루머가 돌았다. 비상위원회에서는 루머를 부인했다. 외신 특파원들이 강제 출국당하기 전에 찍은 것으로 짐작되는 교전 동영상 몇 개가 유투브에 올랐다. 화질은 좋은 편이 아니었지만 AK소총의 딱딱한 폭발음은 또렷이 들렸다. 작은 공장으로 보이는 건물이 굉음과 함께 터졌다. 길쭉한 잿빛 연기가 솟아올랐다. 흔들리는 화면 속에서 사람들이 이리저리 뛰어다녔다. 캐터필러에 짓눌린 시체가 길가에 방치되어 있었다. 블랙은 동영상 중 하나에서 버섯 모양으로 넓게 그늘을 드리운 커다란 느티나무 아래 죽은 사람들이 천에 덮여 누워 있는 광경을 봤다. 여자들이 나

nication tower somewhere might have been de-stroyed.

Or, the phone conversation itself might have been his dream.

The news of the coup d'état was slipping from a headline story to the bottom of the page. There were many other important events to consider be-sides a coup in another country, something that didn't really affect their daily affairs. Prices for goods kept rising. Manufacturing was slumping. A headless body was found in a remote village. At a movie preview a famous actress stepped on to the red carpet without wearing a bra. In Africa, children were starving to death.

The less the world showed interest in the coup, the more available information on it there was. The coup forces instituted an emergency committee and issued a road map declaring their goal: cleanse corruption and the government's unacceptable sta-tus quo, drive out the country's internal enemies through revolutionary measures, maintain a demo-cratic system against outside threats. A rumor was circulating that an airplane with former high gov-ernment officials on board had dove into interna-tional waters due to sudden bout of turbulence.

무 아래에서 통곡하고 있었다. 동영상들은 현재 머물고 있는 지역에서는 볼 수 없다는 공지와 함께 삭제되었다. 비상위원회에서는 민간인 사상자는 없다고 밝혔다.

국장에게서는 그날 이후 연락이 없었다. 블랙은 규정을 어길 각오를 하고 회사 간부들이 사용하는 직통라인으로 전화를 걸었다. 라인 담당자는 그가 하는 모든 질문에 현재는 확인할 수 없으니 현 위치에서 대기하라는 말만 되풀이했다. 개인번호를 아는 몇 안 되는 회사 동료들의 전화기는 꺼져 있거나 메시지를 남기라는 안내 음성만 떴다.

그는 아주 잠깐, 세상의 종말이란 모두가 죽어버리는 게 아니라 이런 식으로 홀로 잊히는 게 아닌가 하는 생각을 했다.

마침내 연락이 온 건 블랙이 예비 여권을 만지작거리며 귀국 루트로 육로가 좋을까 해로가 좋을까 가늠하던 어느 밤이었다.

"현재까지 상황을 보고해 봐."

전화기 너머에서 자기 억양 같은 것에는 조금도 관심이 없는 딱딱하고 단호한 목소리가 말했다. 블랙은 짧고 간결하게 보고했다. 감시는 계속 이루어지고 있으며

The emergency committee denied this rumor. A few video clips that foreign correspondents might have taken before they were expelled were uploaded on YouTube. The video was in poor condition, but one could clearly hear the harsh rattle of AK-47 shots. Buildings that looked like small factories were exploding to an accompaniment of thunderous noises. Gray smoke soared high up into the sky. Shaky camera footage captured scenes of civilians running frantically. Bodies crushed by caterpillars were being abandoned on the streets. In one of the video clips, Black saw covered bodies lying under the shade of a large mushroom-shaped zelkova tree. Women were wailing under the tree. The video clips were soon deleted, leaving only a notice saying that these could not be seen in Black's current country. The emergency committee announced that there were no civilian casualties.

The director had not contacted him since the last time they had spoken. Risking a violation, Black used the hot line only the high officials of his company were allowed to use. The person on the other line repeated the same answer to all his questions: he could not confirm anything at the moment, so Black should continue standing by.

옐로의 일상은 크게 변한 건 없다. 강변. 도서관. 고양이. 분수쇼. 다만 현재의 인력과 상황에서 애초의 임무를 실현하는 건 어려울 수도 있다. 지시를 기다리고 있다.

"임무가 바뀌었다. 예전에 내려온 지시가 뭐였건 간에 잊는다. 이제 목표를 경호한다. 사흘 안에 추가 지원인력이 갈 예정이다. 지원이 도착하면 목표를 귀국시킨다. 자네도 같이 온다. 할 일이 많아."

"목표는 이 사실을 알고 있습니까? 국장님과도 얘기가 된 겁니까? 임무가 이렇게 바뀌는 건……"

"말이라고 하나. 원래 이렇게 말이 많았나?"

"하나만 더 묻겠습니다. 이 회선은 국장님밖에는 모릅니다. 정식으로 인수인계가 이뤄진 상황입니까? 저는 여전히 비선입니까?"

"하나가 아니라 두 개군."

그러더니 갑자기 전화가 끊겼다. 블랙은 잠시 생각에 잠겼다. 정확히 설명할 수 없는 불안감이 목탁을 치듯 가슴 한구석을 톡톡 때렸다. 그는 재빨리 필요한 짐만 챙겨 브라운의 방을 빠져나왔다. 맨션 주변에 아무도 없다는 걸 확인한 뒤에야 그는 자기가 과민반응을 했다는 걸 알았다.

Several colleagues' phones Black knew were either turned off or notified him to leave a message.

For a very brief moment, he thought that the end of the world would not be one where everyone died, but one in which everyone was forgotten or left alone.

Black finally received a call the night he was trying to decide if he should return home by land or by sea. He fumbled his spare passport as he answered his phone.

"Full report requested!" a voice intoned on the other side. The voice did not seem to have any interest whatsoever in varying its tone.

Black reported briefly and concisely. He had kept his eyes on the target and Yellow was maintaining his regular schedule. Riverside. Library. The water fountain show. The only snag in the operations was that it might be difficult for him to execute the original plan in his current situation. He had been standing by.

"Your mission has changed. Dismiss whatever directives you received earlier. You must now guard the target. Additional personnel are scheduled to arrive within three days. Once they arrive, you will guide the target home. You will accompany him. You have a lot to do."

물론 그러는 게 넋 놓고 앉아 있는 것보다는 현명했다.

다음 날 오전 블랙은 옐로의 오피스텔을 찾아갔다. 며칠 동안 훔쳐보기만 했던 건물에 당당히 들어가자니 기분이 이상했다. 문 앞에서 초인종을 누르고 기다렸다. 반응이 없었다. 다시 누르려는데 누군가 그의 팔을 비틀더니 벽에 몸을 짓눌렀다. 딱딱한 뭔가가 오른쪽 옆구리 바로 위쪽 갈비뼈 틈을 쑤셨다.

"대낮부터 간이 부었구나. 누구냐. 누가 보냈어?"

옐로가 말했다. 블랙의 목 뒤에서 노인의 쉰내가 훅 끼쳐왔다. 블랙은 자기 몸을 누르고 있는 물건의 정체를 파악하려고 애썼다. 총? 잭나이프? 길에서 주운 막대기?

"무기는 없습니다."

"그건 내가 판단할 문제고."

옐로가 블랙의 몸을 수색하며 말했다. 그는 마지막으로 블랙의 사타구니를 힘주어 쥐고 나서는 팔을 다시 세게 비틀면서 갖고 있던 물건으로 블랙의 등을 쿡 찔렀다.

"누구냐고 했다."

"연락 못 받으셨습니까?"

"Does the target know this? Has this been discussed with the director? Changing the mission like this..."

"What are you saying? Are you always this talkative?"

"Let me ask you just one more question. Only the director knows this line. Has the work officially transferred? Do I still belong to the secret line?"

"Not one, but two." The phone disconnected.

Black thought about all of this for a while. An uneasy feeling that he could not exactly explain was beating a corner of his chest like a Buddhist wood block. He quickly packed only the bare necessities of his and left Brown's room. After confirming that no one was waiting for him near the building, he realized that he was overreacting.

Of course, that was wiser than just sitting and waiting absentmindedly.

The next morning, Black went to Yellow's office studio. It felt strange to walk openly into the building that he had been secretly watching for days. He rang the bell and waited at the door. No response. When he was about to ring the bell again, someone twisted his arms and pushed his body against the wall. Something hard was poking between his ribs right above his right side.

"연락 같은 소리 하고 있네."

"빌뉴스. 프놈펜. 방첩 스크랩에서 사진을 잘못 보내는 바람에 엉뚱한 사람을 잡을 뻔 했잖습니까. 스쿼시는 포핸드보다 백핸드가 더 나았지요. 커트라인 바로 위를 맞춰서 코너를 찌르는 게 장기 아니었습니까."

블랙의 팔목을 억세게 잡았던 손이 조심스럽게 힘을 뺐다.

"두 손 들어. 뒤로 돌아. 천천히."

블랙은 몸을 돌렸다. 옐로를 이렇게 가까이에서 본 건 임무를 시작하고 나서 처음이었다. 그는 멀리서 지켜봤던 것보다 훨씬 더 늙어 보였다. 그러나 블랙은 그의 얼굴에 그간 없던 활기가 넘쳐 흐른다는 걸 충분히 알아볼 수 있었다. 불만스럽게 축 처졌던 입술은 각진 아래턱과 평행을 이루고 있었고 눈은 반짝였다. 키도 갑자기 반 뼘 쯤 커진 것 같았다.

"온다는 사람이 자네였어?"

옐로의 입가에 큼지막한 미소가 떠올랐다. 그는 오른손에 들고 있던 립밤 뚜껑을 따 입술에 바른 뒤 주머니에 집어넣고는 입술을 안으로 오므렸다 쭉 폈다.

"바나나 맛이야."

"In broad daylight—pretty reckless, huh! Who are you? Who sent you?" Yellow said.

Black could smell an offensive old man musk behind his neck. Black tried to find out what it was that was pressing hard on his body. A gun? A jackknife? A stick he'd picked up on the street?

"I'm unarmed."

"I'm the one who'll see about that," Yellow said, searching Black's body. After getting a vicious grip on Black's groin and forcefully twisting his arms back again, he pushed whatever he was holding into Black's back.

"I asked you who you were."

"You haven't received a call?"

"Call? What call?"

"Vilnius. Phnom Phen. The anti-spy scrapbook division sent the wrong photo and so we almost caught the wrong person. Your backhand was better than your forehand when you played squash, right? Wasn't your specialty throwing to the corner just above the cutline?"

Black could feel the hand twisting his arms carefully loosen its grip.

"Raise both hands. Turn around. Slowly."

Black turned around. This was the first time he had seen Yellow so up close since he had begun

옐로는 그렇게 말하며 혀로 입술을 슬쩍 핥았다.

"생각보다 빨리 나타났기에 난 또 나한테 원한이라도 품은 놈인 줄 알았지. 세상이 이렇다 보니까……."

옐로가 말했다. 블랙은 어깨를 주무르면서 오피스텔 내부를 둘러보았다. 현관문을 지나 싱크대, 전자레인지, 냉장고가 욕실을 마주보는 좁고 짧은 공간을 지나면 방이 나왔다. 벽을 면한 곳에 속이 빈 커다란 상자 모양 공간이 있었고, 그 상자 위에 놓인 매트리스와 베개가 침구였다. 상자 안에는 작은 옷장과 붙박이 책상이 있었다. 창문 바로 옆에 작은 원형 테이블과 구식 브라운관 TV가 놓여 있었고 에어컨은 침대 바로 위에 설치되어 있었다. 오래 지내기보다는 출장 온 비즈니스맨들이 잠시 머물렀다 가기 알맞았다. 평면도를 통해 내부 구조는 파악하고 있었지만 막상 들어와 보니 생각보다 좁았다.

어딘가에서 여자의 신음소리가 들렸다. 옐로가 벽을 부술 듯 두드렸다. 잠시 조용해졌다가 아까보다는 눈치를 보는 것 같은 신음소리가 다시 들렸다.

"이 시간에, 쯧." 옐로가 말했다. 그는 전기주전자에

his mission. Up close, he looked even older. But, Black could recognize a kind of energy radiating from his face unlike before. His lips, which had been drooping unhappily until then, were running parallel with his square chin. His eyes sparkled. He seemed to have suddenly grown taller by half a span.

"You were the one who was supposed to come?"

Yellow smiled brightly. He opened the cover of a container of lip balm he had been holding in his right hand, put it on over his lips, placed it in his pocket, and then sucked his lips in and out.

"Banana taste," Yellow said, smacking his lips lightly.

"Because you showed up earlier than I expected, I thought you were one of my adversaries. I wasn't sure but—the world is what it is…" Yellow said.

Massaging his shoulder, Black took a look around the room. Just inside the door, there was a short, narrow space where the sink, the microwave, and the refrigerator faced a bathroom and then a room. There was a space like a large box next to the wall and there was a mattress and a pillow on top of this box. Inside the box, there was a small closet and a built-in desk. Right next to the window,

물을 부으며 블랙을 흘끗 봤다. "그런데 진짜 어떻게 이리 일찍 왔어? 사흘은 걸릴 거라더니?"

블랙은 미리 생각해뒀던 대답을 했다. 대사관 보안 문제로 출장을 왔다가 쿠데타가 일어나 발이 묶였다. 옐로 얘기는 들어 알았지만 여기 있는 줄은 몰랐다. 신변을 보호하라는 지시를 받고 방문한 것이다. 그 이상은 아직 모른다. 옐로는 고개를 끄덕이면서 전기주전자에서 끓고 있는 물을 커피잔에 부었다.

"내 얘기는 알고 있다는 거지?"

"모를 리가 없지 않겠습니까."

블랙은 그렇게 말하며 붙박이 책상으로 다가갔다. 뉴스를 쭉 체크하고 있었는지 신문기사 스크랩과 인터넷 홈페이지에서 출력한 인쇄물들이 널려 있었다. 비상위원회의 멤버들이 새 정부의 요직에 올랐다는 소식이 맨 위에 놓여 있었다. '되찾은 질서'라는 헤드라인이 달린 기사 사진에서는 활기찬 얼굴의 사람들이 깨끗한 거리 위를 누비면서 안심하고 생업에 종사하는 중이었다. 새 정부가 대규모 집회를 강경하게 진압했다는 외신 기사도 보였다. 기사 사진 속 인적 없는 아스팔트에는 핏자국이 뿌려져 있었다. 노트북 화면에 떠 있는 건 해적 방

there was a small round table and an old-fashioned tube TV. An air-conditioner was just above the bed. This was a place fit for a businessman on a short business trip rather than a room intended for a long-term stay. Although Black knew about its layout through the room's floor plans, he found it much smaller than he had imagined.

Somewhere a woman was moaning. Yellow banged his fist against the wall as if he was trying to knock it down. It became quiet for a moment, but then the moaning started up again, this time a little more subdued than before.

"At this hour, my!" Yellow said. Pouring water into an electric kettle, he glanced at Black. "By the way, how were you able to come so quickly? They told me it would take at least three days."

Black gave him the answer he had already prepared. He had come to the embassy for security purposes before the coup d'état; this prevented him from returning home. He had heard about Yellow, but hadn't known where he was. He had come today because he had been ordered to guard him. He did not know anything else. Yellow nodded and poured the boiling water into a coffee mug.

"You heard about me?"

송 DJ의 블로그였다. DJ의 주장에 따르면 군부는 시위 진압에 실탄을 사용하고 있었으며 이에 맞서는 광범위한 저항의 불길은 꺼질 기미를 보이지 않고 있었다. 그리고 무엇보다, 작은 책상의 대부분을 차지하고 있는, 색색의 파일들과 포스트잇이 마구 붙어 있는 종이가……

"맞아. 자료야." 블랙의 뒤에서 옐로가 말했다. 블랙은 그가 건네주는 뜨거운 커피잔을 잡았다.

"무슨 자료입니까?"

"알면서."

블랙은 어떻게 대답해야 할지 망설였다. 전날의 불안감이 희미하게 되살아났다. 어쩌면 이 대화는 블랙을 테스트하기 위한 함정일지도 몰랐다. 지난밤과 마찬가지로 그런 생각이 과잉반응이라는 건 알았다. 하지만 그것이 그의 삶이었고, 옐로의 삶이기도 했다.

옐로가 계속 말했다.

"모르는 척하긴. 책을 쓰려고 했어, 책. 인터넷에 올리는 건 가짜 같잖아. 책으로 나와야 진짜지. 본때를 보여주고 싶었거든. 자랑은 아니지만 평생 국가에 충성했어. 우리 같은 사람들한테는 당연한 거지. 안 그래? 분

"How could I not?" Black said, and walked to-wards the built-in desk. Yellow had clearly been following the news; cutout newspaper articles and Internet printouts were strewn all over the desk. The news about emergency committee members being appointed government ministers was at the top. In the photo of an article with the headline "Order Regained," people wearing lively expres-sions were walking around clean streets and were safely engaged in their daily occupations. There was a foreign news article that said the new gov-ernment had violently suppressed a massive rally. This article's photo showed a deserted street spot-ted with occasional bloodstains. On Yellow's laptop screen floated a blog from a pirate DJ station. The DJ claimed that the military regime was shooting live rounds to suppress demonstrators but the flames of a massive resistance movement were showing no signs of dying out. Suspended above all of this, there were post-its stuck to a bed of paper and colorful files. Indeed, they took up most of his desk space.

"That's right. Those are the materials," Yellow said from behind Black. Yellow handed him a hot cof-fee.

"What materials?"

수에 안 맞게 출세하려는 욕심도 없었고. 현장에서 구르던 주제에 사무실에 들어왔다고 뒤에서 수군거릴 때도 가만히 있었어. 그런데 날이 갈수록 부패는 심해지고, 다들 잿밥에만 눈을 돌리고. 그것도 좋다 쳐. 그래도 마지막만큼은 날 대우해줘야 하는 거 아냐? 당당히 일해서 떳떳이 받은 표창이야. 그걸 무시해? 그 지부장 새끼, 시험 쳐서 들어와갖고 평생 펜대만 굴렸던 주제에 뭐랬는지 알아? 나보고 예민하대. 생리하냐고. 날 계집년 취급을 했단 말이야. 믿겨져? 그럼 난 어떡하나? 치마라도 걷어올려줘야 하나? 결심을 했지. 오냐, 치마를 걷어주마. 다 까주지. 그 안에 있는 내 좆이나 빨아라. 응? 안 그래?"

블랙은 고개를 끄덕이며 커피를 홀짝였다.

"그러다 세상이 이렇게 바뀌었단 말이야. 회사도 사람이 다 갈렸어. 내 군대 동기가 부장으로 부임한대. 복직이 가능하다고 하네? 횡령사건에 대해서도 책임자를 처벌하겠다고 약속했고. 지금 사람이 부족하대. 혼란기잖아. 경험 많은 인재가 필요한 거지."

"그럴 때지요."

"그런데 그냥은 안 된대. 그래서 내가, 아니 내 능력과

"You know what materials."

Not knowing what would be the best way to respond to that, Black hesitated. The vague uneasy feeling of the previous night returned. This conversation might be a trap to test him. Black knew that he was overreacting like the night before. Still, that was the way of his life, and Yellow's life, too.

Yellow continued, "Don't pretend not to know. I wanted to write a book. A real book, you know. Somehow, writing on the Internet felt fake. A book is real. I wanted to punish them. This isn't something I like to brag about, but I was loyal to my country my entire life. It was a duty for people like us. Right? I didn't have any ambition to overreach beyond what I deserved. I didn't care when people whispered about me behind my back for getting transferred to an office post after some rough work in the field. But, the corruption there was getting really bad and everyone was all so preoccupied with his or her own petty personal gains. Even that would have been okay in the end, though."

"It's just—they should have treated me decently in my last days, right? I worked hard to win that award. I deserved to be proud of it. How could he just ignore that? That branch chief son-of-a-bitch. You know what that exam-passing, pencil-pushing

머리가 있으면 됐지 뭐가 더 필요하냐, 그렇게 말을 했지. 그러니까 내가 뭘 하나 좀 해줘야겠대."

엘로가 장난스러운 미소를 지었다.

"그게 뭡니까?"

"이제 그걸 하러 가는 거야. 마침 딱 맞춰 왔어. 가자고."

엘로가 말했다.

블랙에게는 낯이 익은 삼색털 고양이가 그의 얼굴을 빤히 바라보았다. 그러다 입을 싹 벌리고 하품을 하더니 기지개를 쭉 켜고는 카페 카운터 뒤로 우아하게 돌아가 숨었다.

블랙은 다른 테이블에 있었다. 벽을 등지고 앉았을 때 출입구가 잘 보이는 위치였다. 엘로는 기자와 얘기 중이었다. 오래전에 블랙의 선배 중 하나는 누군가의 직업이란 외모와 행동을 통해 어떻게든 드러나게 마련이라고 했다. 그걸 모르는 건 그저 우리가 그 직업에 대한 지식이 없기 때문일 뿐이라며. 블랙은 기자를 보았다. 뿔테안경 너머의 냉소적인 눈매, 웃지 않는 입매, 담배 냄새, 구부정한 등, 방어적인 자세.

son-of-a-bitch said to me? He said I was sensitive. He asked me if I was on the rag. He treated me like a bitch. Can you believe that joker? So what was I supposed to do? Should I have just lifted up my skirt? I decided. Okay, I'll lift my skirt. I'll show them everything. Suck my dick while you're at it. Huh! Did I do anything wrong?"

Black sipped his coffee and nodded ambiguously.

"Then, suddenly the world turned upside. New personnel started arriving at our company. One of my fellow military alums is going to be director. They told me that they could reinstate me. They also promised me that they would punish the agent responsible for the embezzlement. They need more people. You know it's a confusing time right now. They need experienced talents."

"Of course."

"But, they told me that I couldn't come back for free. So, I asked what more than me, no, my abilities and brain they needed. Then, they told me that I had to do them just one last favor," Yellow said, smiling.

"What do you have to do?"

"I'm on my way to do it right now. You came just in time. Let's go," Yellow said.

나는 저 기자에게 어떻게 보일까?

옐로는 기자 앞에서 몇 시간에 걸쳐 노래를 불렀다. 처음 마주하자마자 옐로는 기자의 직업의식과 언론인으로서의 객관성, 정치적 성향이 궁금하다며 면접 반 심문 반으로 질문을 마구 던졌다. 출신학교, 고향, 아버지 직업, 현 재산, 등등. 그리고 그와 관련된 개똥철학들. 기자의 자질을 확인했다는 판단이 어느 정도 서자 옐로는 지난 정부 시절 진행된 온갖 작전들을 흥얼거리기 시작했다. 기승전결이 뚜렷하고 코러스가 확실한 노래들. 그는 자신이 모은 자료들을 보여주면서 구체적인 작전 내용과 관련 인사들, 명령권자 들의 이름을 읊었다. 운이 좋은 건지 옐로가 신명나게 떠벌리는 작전들 중 블랙이 관여한 건 없었다. 그러나 작전이 하나하나 까발려질 때마다 블랙은 누군가 자신의 뺨을 때리며 옷을 하나씩 벗기는 것 같았다. 역정보, 프락치, 무고, 고문, 증거 조작, 은폐로 점철된 이야기들이 오후의 햇살 아래 천박한 기운을 내뿜었다. 현 정부가 옐로에게 제안한 것은 명확했다. 지난 정부의 작전들을 폭로하라. 그러면 귀국하여 새 정부의 보호 아래 살아가도록 해주겠다. 옐로는 거래를 받아들였고, 새 정부와 관계된 사

The tricolored cat stared at Black. Then, it opened its mouth wide, yawned, straightened its back, gracefully ambled around to the back of the café counter, and then hid.

Black was sitting at another table. He could see the entrance well, sitting with his back against the wall. Yellow was talking with a reporter. A long time ago, one of Black's *seonbaes* said that people were bound to show what they did for living through their appearances and actions. If we couldn't figure them out, then it was simply because we didn't know much about the work they did. Black looked at the reporter. Cynical eyes behind horn-framed glasses, unsmiling lips, a cigarette smell, slightly bent back, defensive posture...

How would I look to that reporter?

Yellow sang for hours in front of the reporter. As soon as Yellow met him, he asked the reporter a number of random questions about his professionalism, journalistic objectivity, and political inclinations. It was as if he was interviewing or interrogating him. He asked the reporter what schools he had gone to, where he was from, what his father did, how many assets he had now. He offered his personal philosophy about all of them etc. etc.

When Yellow felt that he had confirmed the re-

항들을 교묘하게 건너뛰어 가면서 자기가 아는 거의 모든 내용을 털어놓고 있었다. 기자가 이 이야기들이 사실임을 입증할 수 있느냐고 물었다. 옐로는 증거들을 보고도 그런 말이 나오느냐며 필요하다면 기자회견이건 무엇이건 할 거라고 핏대를 올렸다.

그는 자기가 지금껏 제일 잘해 온 일을 정말로 잘하고 있었다.

옐로의 노래를 듣는 동안 블랙은 자신의 옛 상관이 살아남을 수 없으리라는 걸 확신했다. 곧 도착한다는 지원인력들은 공해상 밖에 있는 산호초 틈새에 그의 묏자리를 마련해 놓았을 것이다. 어쩌면 사정을 대충 파악하고 있는 블랙 본인의 것도. 설사 지원인력들이 옐로를 귀국시킨다 하더라도 일이 이렇게 된 이상 전 정부의 사람들이 옐로를 가만 놔둘 리가 없었다. 하지만 누가 손에 피를 묻히건 그의 죽음은 부패한 전 정부의 복수로 비칠 것이다. 새 정부에게는 어느 쪽이건 남는 장사였다. 블랙은 옐로가 이 간단한 계산을 못한다는 걸 믿을 수 없었다. 귀국에 대한 갈망과 손상된 명예에 대한 집착이 경험 많은 베테랑의 눈을 가리고 있었다. 블랙이 봤다고 생각했던 빛은 그의 내면에서 나오던 게

porter's character, he began to launch into all the operations the company had carried out under the previous government. Yellow's stories were little songs with clear, tight structures and four parts – an introduction, development, climax, and conclusion—and then the chorus. Yellow showed the reporter all materials he himself had collected, recited the names of relevant people and officers in charge and personnel issuing orders, and, finally, provided all specifics of individual operations as well. Perhaps, because Black was lucky, he hadn't been involved in any of those operations Yellow was going on about. But, every time Yellow exposed an operation, Black felt as if he was being slapped across the face, divested of his clothes, piece by piece. The stories of counter-intelligence work, undercover work, false accusations, fabricated evidence, and cover-ups were gushing out obscenely under the afternoon sunlight. It was clear what the current government had offered Yellow. Expose everything he knew about operations under the previous regime and the new government would guarantee his protection and safe return home. Yellow had accepted the deal and divulged almost everything he knew, cleverly avoiding details related to the new government. The reporter

아니라 그를 가리고 있던 희망의 장막에서 반사된 것이었고 그를 감싸는 활기는 덫을 보지 못하고 먹이에 달려드는 짐승의 성급함에 다름 아니었다. 블랙은 자신이 임무에서 완전히 해방되었음을 알았다. 이 일은 그를 떠난 것이었다.

하지만 그는 조금도 개운하지 않았다.

인터뷰가 끝난 뒤 옐로는 블랙을 근처 술집으로 데려갔다. 그는 한껏 흥이 올라 크게 웃고 신나게 떠들었다. 그러다 테이블 옆을 지나가던 종업원의 엉덩이를 툭툭 쳤다. 종업원이 기분 나쁜 표정을 짓자 옐로는 화를 냈고, 급기야 술집 주인과 드잡이까지 했다. 블랙은 겨우 그를 떼어 말렸다.

"돈 받고 장사하는 새끼들이 말이야."

옐로가 씩씩거렸다.

그들은 술집을 나와 편의점에 가 진열대를 털다시피 맥주를 샀다. 옐로가 이대로 끝낼 수 없다고 해서였다. 오피스텔로 돌아온 그들은 원형 테이블 위에 맥주캔들을 쌓아놓고 술을 마셨다. 옐로는 좋았던 옛 시절 얘기를 늘어놓았고, 블랙은 맥주를 찔끔거리면서 맞장구를 쳤다.

asked Yellow if he could prove all of these stories. Yellow asked him how he could ask him something like that after seeing all the evidence Yellow had just presented him. Yellow almost angrily added that he would do whatever it took to corroborate his stories, including holding a press conference.

Yellow was doing well what he had done best during his entire career.

As Black listened to Yellow's little songs, he was sure that his old superior wouldn't survive this. The backup personnel about to arrive must have prepared his grave among the coral reefs in international waters. They might have already prepared Black's grave as well because he knew the state of affairs so well. Even if the backup personnel took Yellow home, there was no way the people of the previous regime would leave him alone in this situation. Nevertheless, no matter whose hand was bloodied, his death would look like an act of vengeance by the previous regime. The new government wouldn't lose anything however Yellow died. Black could not believe that Yellow could not see this simple arithmetic. His yearning for home and his obsession with his wounded pride and honor were blinding the eyes of this highly experienced veteran. The light Black had thought he'd seen

"내가 오늘 큰일을 했어. 내일이면 세상이 바뀐다고."

"축하드립니다."

블랙이 말했다.

"축하할 일이지. 더 마실 거지? 더 마셔야지!"

옐로가 화장실에 간 사이 블랙은 TV를 켰다. 색색의 비키니를 입은 여자들이 끈끈한 녹색 젤을 채운 고무풀장 안에서 육탄전을 벌이고 있었다. 방청석에 앉아 있는 남자들이 박장대소를 하며 뒤집어졌다.

"이 나라는 천박해." 옐로가 또 캔을 따며 말했다. "부끄러운 게 뭔지를 몰라."

블랙은 말없이 TV를 봤다. 프로그램이 끝나고 광고가 번쩍거렸다. 뉴스가 시작되었다. 유통기한이 지난 냉동 닭을 팔던 업자들이 검거되었다는 뉴스가 끝나자 국제뉴스로 넘어갔다. 블랙의 고국 소식이 첫 꼭지였다. 불안한 정국상황 속에서 내전이 발발할 가능성이 여전히 높으며, 전 정부의 인사들이 호시탐탐 복귀를 노리고 있는 가운데 전 정부와 현 정부 양쪽 모두에 저항하는 민병대가 조직되었다는 내용이었다. 민병대의 부대장으로 짐작되는 복면을 쓴 남자가 자신들은 가족을 잃었다며 절대 복수를 포기하지 않을 거라는 인터뷰

from Yellow was not coming from within Yellow himself, it was a reflection from the curtain of hope blinding him. The energy surrounding him was nothing other than the rashness of an animal rushing to food without noticing the snare. Black realized that he had been completely freed from his mission. The work had left him.

Black wasn't feeling all that great about it, though.

After the interview, Yellow took Black to a nearby tavern. Yellow was extremely excited, laughing and talking without a care in the world. He tapped a waitress' hip lightly as she walked by. When she frowned and turned to protest, Yellow got angry and ended up in a near fistfight with the tavern owner. Black barely managed to hold them apart.

"Aren't they merchants? Aren't they supposed to sell what they've got?" Yellow was still fuming.

After they left the tavern they went to a convenience store and bought nearly all the beer on the shelf. Yellow insisted that their day could not end like this. They went back to his room, stacked the beer cans on the round table, and drank. Yellow was talking about the good old days, and Black chimed in from time to time as he sipped beer.

"I did a great job today. The world should be upside down by tomorrow."

를 했다.

복면을 써도, 소총을 어깨에 메도, 브라운은 똑같았
다. 말투에는 그 동안의 고충을 짐작케 하는 무게가 실
려 있었지만 손은 계속해서 복면의 실밥을 잡아뜯고 있
었고 말에는 조리가 없었으며 카메라와는 끝내 눈을 마
주치지 못했다.

형님이라 불러도 되죠?

"배신자들. 거지새끼들." 옐로가 말했다. 이미 술기운
이 꽤 올라 의자 등받이에 몸을 느슨하게 기대고 있었
고 캔을 들지 않은 팔을 축 늘어뜨리고 있었다. "살려둬
서는 안 되지. 저런 새끼들은 싹 쓸어버려야 돼."

"가족을 잃은 사람들입니다."

블랙은 겨우 입을 열었다.

"가족은 나도 잃었어. 누구나 가족을 잃어. 아. 자넨
가족이 없지? 없는 게 나아. 날 봐. 마누라는 암으로 뒈
지고 딸년은 흰둥이와 눈이 맞아 달아났지. 딸년은 날
똥으로 봐. 코끼리 똥으로는 커피라도 만드는데 난 아
무 쓸모가 없다 그러고…… 나쁜 년."

옐로가 TV를 턱짓으로 가리켰다.

"그거 알아? 돌아가면 저것들부터 처리할 거야. 어떻

"Congratulations, sir!" Black said.

"It's worth the congratulations. Another drink? Of course, you'll have another!"

While Yellow was in the bathroom, Black turned on his TV. Women in colorful bikinis were wrestling each other in an elastic pool filled with green gel. Men were applauding and laughing in the audience.

"This country is shallow," Yellow said, opening a beer can. "They don't know shame."

Black watched the TV without saying another word. The program ended and a commercial flashed across the screen. The news began. After news about dealers getting arrested for selling frozen chicken past their due dates, the international news appeared. New information about Black's home country was the first item. The news anchor said that the political situation was unstable, the possibility of the civil war was still high, and the former regime officials were trying to make a comeback while militia corps resisting both the former and the present governments had begun organizing. A man wearing a mask, presumably a militia commander, informed an interviewer that he had already lost his entire family and that he would never give up until he had his revenge.

게 하는지 알려줄까? 진짜 쉬워. 뼈다귀 몇 개만 던져주
면 알아서 물고 뜯다 자폭한다고. 근데 그러고 보니 자
네는 왜 가족이 없어? 그 나이 먹도록. 혹시 자네……
어라, 응? 그런 거야?"

옐로는 자기 농담을 미처 다 즐기지 못했고, 그럴 리
도 없었겠지만, 사과할 시간도 갖지 못했다. 블랙이 순
식간에 일어나 옐로의 가슴을 발로 찼기 때문이었다.
옐로는 의자에 앉은 채 그대로 넘어갔다. 반격할 틈을
주지 말아야 했다. 블랙은 TV의 볼륨을 잽싸게 끝까지
올린 다음 테이블을 들어 옐로를 내리찍었다. 옐로는
막으려고 손을 치켜들었지만 술에 취해 반응이 느렸다.
테이블이 노인의 가슴과 목 사이를 강타했다. 옐로가
몸을 웅크리며 숨을 쉬려고 꺽꺽대는 사이 블랙은 베개
아래에 손을 넣었다. 이 방에 총이 있다면 거기뿐이었
다. 없다면? 이 노인의 완력을 당할 수 있을까? 글록의
두툼한 손잡이가 착 달라붙듯 잡혔다. 블랙은 목에 걸
린 호루라기를 불려고 애쓰던 옐로의 머리에 베개를 덮
는 것과 동시에 숨을 멈추고 방아쇠를 재빨리 두 번 당
겼다. 어깨를 때리는 반동과 함께 두개골이 깨지는 느
낌이 손끝을 통해 전해졌다.

Although he was wearing a mask and holding a rifle under his shoulder, there was no mistaking that it was Brown. His voice carried a weight that showed his pain, but he picked at his mask, his sentences illogical, while avoiding eye contact with the camera.

May I call you *hyeongnim*?

"Traitors! Bums!" Yellow said.

Already quite drunk, Yellow leaned in the back of the chair and his free hand lay on the side of his chair listlessly. "We shouldn't let them live! We should wipe all those sons-of-bitches out!"

"They lost their families," Black barely managed to open his mouth.

"I lost my family, too. Everyone loses his or her family. Oh, you don't have a family? Be grateful. Look at me. My wife died of cancer, and my bitch of a daughter ran off with a whitie. That bitch thinks I'm a shit. Told me that we can at least make coffee out of the elephant shit, but I'm useless. And... Bitch!"

Yellow pointed at the TV with his chin and said, "Do you know? I'm going to take care of them first thing as soon as I return home. Do you want to know how I'm going to do it? Easy. If we throw them a few bones, they'll fight among themselves

블랙은 옐로의 몸을 타고 앉아 숨을 몰아쉬며 바닥에 번지는 피를 바라보았다. 베개를 소음기로 썼지만 총소리를 완전히 가리진 못했다. 오전의 신음소리를 고려해보면 이 건물의 벽은 무척 얇았다. 아래층 사람들은 천장을 강타한 충격 때문에 놀랐을 것이다. 누군가는 벌써 경찰에 전화를 걸었을지도 모른다.

장비 없이 가능할까?

몇 분 뒤 오피스텔 건물 전체에 화재경보가 울렸다. 놀란 사람들이 서둘러 옷을 챙겨입고 방에서 뛰쳐나왔다. 몇몇은 속옷 바람으로 허둥댔다. 어차피 더운 밤이었다. 사람들 틈에 섞여 건물을 빠져나온 블랙은 조용히 그곳을 벗어났다.

그는 조금 들뜬 기분으로 밤거리를 배회했다. 그러다 가장 먼저 눈에 띈 공중전화로 들어가 간부용 직통라인으로 전화를 걸었다. 졸음이 덜 가신 목소리로 전화를 받은 담당자에게 임무를 완수했다고 보고한 뒤 대답을 기다리지 않고 끊었다. 그런 다음 뒷일에 대한 걱정은 잠시 내려놓은 채 밤공기를 만끽하며 맨션까지 걸어갔다. 골목을 돌고 다리를 건넜다. 강변에 늘어선 포장마차에서 숯불에 구운 꼬치와 돼지 뼈를 고아 만든 국물

and collapse from the inside. But, by the way, why don't you have a family? At your age? Perhaps, you... Oh! Wait! Are you that...?"

Yellow couldn't enjoy his joke much, and he didn't have time to apologize even if he'd wanted to – which was highly unlikely anyway. Black got up and kicked Yellow in the chest. Yellow fell backwards along with the chair he'd been sitting on. Black had to deny him any opportunity to fight back. Black quickly turned the TV volume up to maximum, lifted the table up high and brought it straight down on Yellow. Although Yellow tried to fight back, raising his arms uselessly in defense, he was drunk and his responses were slow. The table struck the old man hard between his chest and neck. While Yellow crouched and tried hard to gather his breath, Black put his hand under the pillow. He thought that if there was a gun, it had to be there. If not? Could he beat the old man physically? The thick handle of a Glock fit his hand perfectly, as if it was attracted to his hand. As Black put the pillow over Yellow's head, who was trying desperately to use the whistle around his neck, Black held his breath and quickly pulled the trigger twice. Along with the feeling of the gun's rebound hitting his shoulder, the feeling of Yellow's skull splintering

냄새가 솔솔 풍겼다. 유흥가의 불빛들이 강물 표면에서 반짝였다. 높은 빌딩들 사이에서 더운 바람이 불었다. 잎이 무성한 가로수가 싸리비를 쓸듯 부스스 소리를 내며 가지를 떨었다. 다리 끝에서 블랙은 뒤를 돌아보았다. 어딘가에서 불이 난 것 같았다. 하지만 불꽃도 연기도 보이지 않았다. 소방차의 사이렌 소리도 들리지 않았다.

* 이베리아의 전설에는 전갈이 불길에 휩싸이면 자신의 꼬리에 있는 독침으로 자살한다는 이야기가 있다. 1883년에 영국에서 이루어진 한 실험에서 전갈을 유리병 안에 넣은 뒤 열을 가하고 전기충격을 주는 등의 자극을 가하자 전갈이 자신을 찌르는 장면이 관찰되었다. 그러나 이후 프랑스 연구진의 실험 결과 전갈의 독은 자신에게는 듣지 않는다는 사실이 밝혀졌다.
* 이 소설의 원제목은 이베리아의 전갈이었으나 작가가 영문판에는 "Dishonored"로 새로 제목을 달았다.

traveled up Black's fingertips. Black sat on top of Yellow's body and looked at the blood spreading on the floor. He tried to calm his breathing. Although he had used the pillow as a silencer, he could not muffle the sound of the shots completely. Considering the moaning sounds he had heard that morning, the walls of this building were clearly pretty thin. The people living downstairs must have been surprised by the impact on their ceiling. Somebody could have already called the police.

Could he do it without devices?

A few minutes later, the fire alarm went off in the entire building. Alarmed, people ran out the building after hastily putting on whatever clothes they could find. A few emerged flustered and only in their underwear. It was a hot night any way. Black came out with the crowd and left the area quietly.

He wandered around the night streets feeling mildly elated. He went to the first telephone booth he ran into and called the hot line. He reported to the clerk at the other end that he had accomplished his mission and hung up without waiting for any response. Then, forgetting about the aftermath of what he had done, he walked in the direction of his apartment. He took a deep breath of the night air. He turned a corner and crossed a bridge.

Smells of barbequed food on skewers and the broth made of pork bones wafted through the air from the covered cart bars lining the riverbank. Lights from the entertainment district were sparkling over the river. A hot breeze was blowing between the tall buildings. The branches of the roadside trees were trembling with a rustling sound like the sound of a sweeping besom broom. Black turned around when he reached the end of the bridge. It seemed that a fire had started somewhere. But he could not see any flames or smoke. He couldn't hear any sirens, either.

* In Iberian myth, scorpions would kill themselves with their own poisonous stingers when subjected to heat and fire. In 1883, this belief was apparently confirmed when English researchers observed a scorpion prick itself with its own stinger after being subjected to heat and electric shock treatment. However, it was later discovered by French scientists that a scorpion's poison was ineffective to itself.

* This short story's original Korean title is "An Iberian Scorpion," but the author re-titled it into "Dishonored" in English.

Translated by Jeon Seung-hee

창작노트
Writer's Note

이 단편은 계간《문학동네》의 청탁을 받고 썼다. 대개의 이야기가 그렇겠지만 이 소설 역시 청탁을 받은 순간부터 준비, 땅! 하는 식으로 시작된 건 아니다. 그럼 어디까지 거슬러 올라가야 할까? 소설 첫머리에 블랙이 옐로를 감시하는 장면은 일본 후쿠오카 현 하카타 시의 호텔 겸 쇼핑몰인 캐널시티 하카타에 머물렀을 때 본 분수 쇼의 기억에서 나온 것이다. 도호쿠 대지진과 후쿠시마 원전 사고가 터지기 반년 전이었다. 공기는 뜨거웠고 하늘은 더할 나위 없이 맑았으며 굵은 설탕이 바닥에 깔린 카스텔라는 달콤했다. 기차에 앉아 뭔가를 써 보면 멋질 것 같아서 가져간 노란 표지의 갱지 노트

I wrote this short story thanks to a request from the literary magazine, *Munhakdongne*. Like most stories, I did not begin to write this story the moment I was asked to write with "Ready-Set-Go!" When did I really start? The scene in the beginning of the story, when Black is keeping an eye on Yellow, originated from my memory of a water fountain show I saw when I stayed in the Canal City Hakata, a hotel and shopping complex in Fukuoka, Japan. This happened half year before the Tohoku earthquake and the Fukushima nuclear disaster. The air was hot, the sky was magnificently clear, and the castella sponge cake, sitting atop a bed of coarse-grained sugar, was sweet. The rough paper

는 결국 도시락 받침대가 되었다.

다시 갈 기회가 있을까?

이후 지난해 여름 여러 명의 주인공이 나오는 장편을 굴려보던 중 모종의 실수를 저질러 해외지부로 밀려난 정보기관원을 등장시키자는 아이디어가 떠올랐다. 그는 그곳에서 재기의 기회를 노리고 있으며, 우연한 기회에 사건의 진행에 영향을 끼치는 결정적인 단서를 잡는다. 머릿속에서는 꽤 멋진 착상처럼 보였지만 막상 한 장(章) 정도 분량의 스케치를 해보니 전체의 흐름과는 어울리지 않았을 뿐더러 굳이 넣을 필요도 없었다. 상상이라는 무균실에서 배양된 아이디어는 현실의 공기를 쐬면 종종 다루기 힘든 이상한 모습으로 변하곤 한다. 이 경우도 그랬다. 하지만 이미 그때부터 내심 이것을 독립된 단편으로 바꾸면 좋겠다는 생각을 품었던 것 같다. 그려놓은 밑그림이 있으니 살을 붙이고 다듬고…… 뭐 그러면 되지 않겠어? 단편 하나 날로 먹는 건 일도 아니다 이거지.

그런 생각조차도 무균실 아이디어였다는 것을 곧 깨달았다.

notebook with its yellow cover I'd brought along with me—thinking that it would be nice to write something in a train—ended up as a tray for my bento box.

Will I have an opportunity to revisit that place?

Last summer, when I was trying to come up with a story for a novel with multiple main characters I hit upon the idea to feature an intelligence agent who'd been transferred to an overseas branch for a certain mistake he'd made. This character tries to find an opportunity to return when he happens to find a clue critical to his plan. Although this sounded like a great idea when I first imagined it, I realized after writing about a page draft that it did not fit with the overall structure of the novel in progress and I did not need it for the novel after all. Often times, the ideas I cultivate in the sterilized room called imagination change into strange new things after they're exposed to the outside air. It was true in this case as well. I think I began thinking about turning it into a short story then. Since I'd already written a draft, I could flesh it out and tinker around with it... That could work, right? I could get a short story out of it for free then, right?

I soon realized that this kind of idea had also come from the sterilized room.

스파이 소설에 대해서는 늘 아스라한 낭만을 갖고 있다. 더 정확히 말하면 존 르 카레(John Le Carre)나 로버트 리텔(Robert Littell) 등이 바꿔놓은 게임의 규칙을 따르는 소설이나 영화에 대한 낭만이다. 그런 소설들에서 슈퍼맨 같은 첩보요원은 등장하지 않는다. 머리도 좋고 완력도 있지만 세상을 뒤엎을 정도는 아니며, 설사 그가 없다고 해서 일이 안 돌아가는 것도 아니다. 진짜 중요한 건 시스템이다. 시스템은 허점도 많고 멍청한 짓도 자주 하지만 인간들을 내칠 때만큼은 빈틈없고 냉정하다. 신기하게도 그렇다.

　사정이 그렇다 보니 '현대적'인 스파이 소설들은 은근히 하드보일드 미스터리를 닮아 있는 것처럼 보일 때가 있다. 『팅커, 테일러, 솔저, 스파이』의 조지 스마일리가 벌이는 끈질긴 탐색이야말로 로스 맥도널드(Ross Mac Donald)의 소설에 나오는 탐정 루 아처가 하는 일 아니겠는가? 그런 맥락에서 '현대적'인 스파이 소설이나 영화에서 가끔 유난스럽다 싶게 격렬히 터져 나오는 감상주의는 시스템의 비정함에 대한 인간적인 탄식 아닐까? 오히려 '구식' 첩보원이 나오는 제임스 본드 영화 속에서 별다른 신파적 감상이 느껴지지 않는 건 그 때문

I had always had vague romantic yearnings to write spy fiction. More accurately, I had a yearning to write a story that followed the rules of the game that John le Carré or Robert Littell had changed completely. Their novels never featured Superman-like intelligence agents. They were smart and strong, but they didn't have the power to turn their worlds upside down. Things in the world would be just fine without them. What really mattered was the system. Although the system had holes and was often the perpetrator of ridiculous acts, it was decisive and coldhearted when it tossed human beings aside. This fact was almost surprisingly refreshing.

As this is the current status of the "modern" spy novel, they seem quite similar to the hardboiled mystery. Isn't George Smiley's dogged search in *Tinker Taylor Soldier Spy* the same as private detective Lew Archer's work in Ross MacDonald's novels? In this context, isn't the sentimentalism that occasionally bursts forth in "modern" spy novels or movies the human sigh of an audience or artist in reaction to the cold-heartedness of our system? Isn't that the reason why we cannot feel much sentimentalism in the "old-fashioned" James Bond movies? In those movies, James Bond is probably

이 아닐까? 거기서 본드는 시스템의 일부라기보다는 시스템 그 자체, 또는 시스템의 이상적 화신처럼 움직이고 있는지도 모른다.

물론 이 모든 것들은 실제 현실을 반영한다기보다는 예술적 선택과 조작, 그리고 일정하게 의도된 (반[反] 카타르시스를 포함한) 카타르시스의 산물일 것이다. 이안 플레밍(Ian Fleming)이나 존 르 카레가 첩보 업무를 수행했던 경험을 바탕으로 소설을 썼다 해도 그 사실이 변하지는 않는다. 그리고 그걸 수용하는 한국의 독자나 관객들은 최소한 세 겹의 안경, 즉 다른 언어와 다른 지리, 다른 역사라는 안경을 쓴 채 그걸 읽고 본다. 내가 느꼈던 '아스라한' 낭만도 거기서 왔을지 모른다. 흥미로운 건 창작자도 이 안경을 쓰고 무언가를 만든 듯 보일 때가 있다는 것이다. 이 단편을 쓰기 전에 류승완 감독의 영화 〈베를린〉을 봤는데, 그 영화에서 바로 그런 기분을 느꼈다. 영화 제작 과정에서 류승완 감독은 실제 남북한 스파이들의 세계를 꼼꼼하게 취재했다고 한다. 이는 다시 말하자면 그런 느낌이 드는 게 리얼리티의 문제가 아니라는 뜻 아닐까. 픽션과 현실은 우리가 직관적으로 생각하는 것보다 훨씬 더 다른 점이 많은

acting not as a part of the system, but is acting as the system itself, the ideal incarnation of the system.

Of course, all these are not reflections of reality, but the products of artistic choices and manipulations, of catharsis (including anti-catharsis) intended in a certain way. This is true even if Ian Fleming or John le Carré wrote novels based on their actual spy experiences. Korean readers and audience read and watch their novels and movies wearing at least three interpretative lenses: the lens of a different language, the lens of a different geography, and the lens of a different history. The vague romantic yearning I felt probably came from distance between these three views. Interestingly enough, even the creators sometimes seem to wear these glasses when they craft their products. Before I wrote this short story, this is what I felt when watching *The Berlin File* by Ryoo Seung-wan. I heard that the director himself had actually conducted meticulous research on the actual lives of South Korean and North Korean spies during the production of the film. Perhaps this means that the feeling of distance has nothing to do with reality itself? The world of fiction and the real world might be far more different than we naturally assume. For

세계일지도 모른다. 이를테면 최근 정보기관과 관련하여 세상을 떠들썩하게 하고 있는 논란을 보며 새삼 실감하는 점은 스파이 일이라는 것이 어떤 누군가에게는 궁극적으로 월급을 받고 하는 업무 이상도 이하도 아니라는 사실이다. 지루하고 반복적이며, 의미를 찾기 어렵고, 때로는 영 내키지 않을 수도 있지만, 생계와 가정을 꾸리기 위해 해야 하는 업무.

그러나 그 업무가 불러일으키는 파장은 그렇지 않다.

이 단편 역시 실제 현실을 참고하긴 했지만 반영하거나 논평하지는 않았다. 서두에서 작가들이 종종 쓰듯, '이 소설의 내용은 완전한 허구이며 혹시 소설의 내용이 실제의 인물이나 사건과 겹친다면 그건 전적으로 우연입니다.' 전문적인 관점과 태도로 쓴 스파이 소설도 아니다. 그보다는 두꺼운 안경을 쓰고 읽었던 스파이 소설에 대한 짧고 서투른 독후감에 가깝다고 생각한다.

공개된 지면에 발표한 건 이 단편이 두 번째지만, 다른 많은 작가들도 그럴 것이라 믿는데, 그 이전에 쓰고 버린 습작들이 많이 있게 마련이다. 거기까지 셈을 쳐서 말한다면 이 단편은 나로서는 처음 써본 종류의 것

example, watching the recent political scandals and controversies involving the South Korean intelligence agency, I realize once again that spy work is ultimately nothing more, nor less, than the ordinary work one does to make a living. It's the kind of work that must be done by its agents in order to make a living for themselves and their families, although it is boring, repetitive, meaningless, and sometimes fairly unappealing.

Still, the influence of this kind of work is another story.

I referred to reality to write this short story – although I did not reflect or comment on it. As writers often write in the beginning of their stories, "This story is purely a work of fiction, any connection it may have to real people or incidents is entirely coincidental." This was not spy fiction written from the perspective of a professional. Instead, I believe this story is closer to a short, awkward book report written after reading spy novels through a pair of thick lenses.

Although this is my second book of published short stories, like most writers I have written and discarded many other pieces. Amongst all of these literary efforts, this is my first attempt at this kind of

이다. 그러니까 '도시'나 '회사' 등으로 모호하게 표기되는 공간을 배경으로 '블랙'이나 '옐로'라는 이름을 가진 사람들이 나오는 이야기 말이다. 스파이들의 코드명을 떠올리며 만든 이름들은 아니다. 색깔로 등장인물을 구분할 때 생길 수 있는 효과들을 시험해 보고 싶었던 건데, 내가 아는 한에서는 폴 오스터(Paul Auster)가 「유령들」에서 시도해 본 방식이기도 하다. 당연히 오스터와 비교하는 건 언감생심이다. 나로서는 성공 여부를 떠나 단편이기 때문에 이렇게 써볼 수 있었던 것이라 생각한다. 중편이나 장편이었다면 내 능력으로는 어조와 분위기를 끝까지 유지하기 어려웠을 것이다.

fiction—one in which the backdrop is only vaguely suggested—the characters living in a "city" and working at a "company," and the characters employing names like "Black" and "Yellow." I chose to give them these names not because they were typical spy codenames. I wanted to experiment with the effect of differentiating characters by color. Paul Auster had already tried this experiment in his *Ghosts*. Of course, I do not mean to compare my short story with Auster's novel. Whether it was a successful experiment or not, I was able to try my hand at this because it was a short story. I probably could not have maintained the same tone and atmosphere if this were a novella or a novel.

해설
Commentary

시스템과 자유

이경재 (문학평론가)

우리는 자유로운가? 방현석의『그들이 내 이름을 부를 때』(이야기공작소, 2012)에서처럼, 차라리 벌레가 되지 못하고 인간이 되었음을 저주해야 하는 고문이 국가권력에 의해 벌어지지는 않는다는 점에서 우리는 자유로울지도 모른다. 혹은 이청준의『소문의 벽』(문학과지성사, 1971)에서 정체 모를 사나이들이 등장하여 한밤중에 전깃불로 얼굴을 비추며 너는 좌냐 우냐를 묻는 것과 같은 극단적인 이념적 폭력이 일어나지는 않는다는 점에서 우리는 자유롭다고 말할 수 있을지 모른다. 그러나 다시 한번 묻고 싶다. 갈수록 공고해지는 이 자본주의적 시스템 속에서 우리는 과연 자유로운가?

System and Freedom

Lee Kyung-jae (literary critic)

Are we free? We may be free in the sense that we are not subject to capital torture as we are in Bang Hyun-seok's *When They Call My Name* (Iyagi-gongjakso, 2012); in Bang's work the protagonist endures treatment so harsh he finds himself ultimately willing to forfeit his very humanity, at one point preferring the fate of a caterpillar to that of a human being. Or we may consider ourselves free because unidentified men do not visit us in the middle of night as they do in Yi Cheong-jun's *The Wall of Rumors* (Munji, 1971). The characters of Yi's story find themselves subject to men shining electric lights in their faces and battered them with questions concerning whether they belong to the right

최민우의 「이베리아의 전갈」(《문학동네》, 2013년 여름호)은 과연 감시와 통제가 일상화되고 자본주의적 시스템이 쇠우리처럼 정교해진 현대사회에서 진정한 자유란 가능한 것인가를 옐로, 블랙, 브라운이라는 세 명의 국가정보원을 통하여 묻고 있다. 국가정보기관원이야말로 폐쇄된 시공에서 자신들이 통제할 수 없는 원인에 의해 촉발된 행동을 기계적으로 수행할 뿐, 왜 그런 행동을 해야 하는가의 질문에 대해서는 어떠한 자유도 누릴 여지가 없다는 점에서, 근본적인 자유로부터 소외된 현대인의 전형적인 형상인지도 모른다.

옐로는 평생을 정보기관에서 무탈하게 근무하여 해외 지부의 책임자로 평화로운 퇴직만이 남아 있는 상황에서 전임 지부장에게 모욕을 당한 후, 국가정보기관(작품에서는 회사)과 정면으로 맞선다. 회사는 옐로에게 청구를 철회할지 품위유지 규정위반으로 정직 처분을 받아 연금을 날릴지 선택할 것을 제안하지만, 옐로는 언론에 공금 횡령과 지부의 다른 부패까지 모두 폭로하는 제3의 길을 선택한다. 그 후 옐로는 범죄인 인도협정이 체결되지 않은 나라로 몸을 피해, 기밀 해제도 안 된 이전 작전에 대한 것도 책으로 출판할 계획이다.

or to the left. Still, I'd like to ask, "Are we really free within this ever-intensifying capitalist system?"

Choi Min-woo "Dishonored (*Munhakdongne*, summer 2013)," asks just this kind of question, asking the reader if we can be truly free in our contemporary world, a world in which we are subject to surveillance and control everywhere and at every hour of the day, a world in which our capitalist system has become as elaborate and strong as an iron cage. Interestingly, "Dishonored" chooses to delve into this issue with an in-depth look at the actual agents within this system, intelligence officers known only to the reader as Yellow, Black, and Brown. In this way, Choi's work allows us to see these, and other national security intelligence officers, as typical, alienated modern men, individuals mechanically performing duties defined by causes they cannot control, within closed spaces and times, performing tasks even as they are unable to enjoy the freedom to ask why they are performing them.

"Dishonored" begins with Yellow squarely confronting these nebulous state intelligence agencies ("the company") after what he believes is an inexcusable slight committed by a predecessor and institution completely blind to his work. Prior to this, Yellow had been transferred to a cushy overseas

옐로는 정보원 출신답게 자신의 경호에 철저하지만, 자신의 목을 노리는 암살자는 다름 아닌 옐로 자신이다. 고국에서 쿠데타가 발발하자 모든 상황은 변한다. 회사는 기자 앞에서 지난 정부의 치부를 폭로한다는 조건으로 옐로를 복직시켜 주겠다고 제안하고, 옐로는 이를 받아들인다. 옐로는 기자 앞에서 지난 정부 시절 진행된 "역정보, 프락치, 무고, 고문, 증거 조작, 은폐로 점철된 이야기"(60쪽)들을 흥얼거린다. 이것은 블랙의 생각처럼, 자신의 죽음을 부르는 일이다. 지난 정권의 사람들은 당연히 옐로를 죽이려 할 것이다. 쿠데타로 정권을 잡은 사람들 역시 옐로의 죽음은 이전 정부의 복수로 비칠 것이기 때문에, 옐로의 죽음을 막을 아무런 이유가 없다. 귀국에 대한 갈망과 손상된 명예에 대한 집착이 "부술 수 있는 조직은 몽땅"(22쪽) 파괴하는 파괴공작의 달인이었던 옐로로 하여금 스스로를 파괴하게 만든 것이다.

옐로에게 정보원으로서의 일이란 먹고 살기 위한 직업에 불과하다. 그에게 사명감이나 충성같은 것은 하나의 장식에 지나지 않는다. 그러하기에 자신의 자존심에 작은 상처를 준 농담 하나 때문에 옐로는 조직 전체를

post, a reward just before his retirement and after a lifelong uneventful service. But Yellow's predecessor diminishes his achievement with an offhand remark, prompting Yellow to fly into a rage at public company event. Further exacerbating matters for Yellow, the company presents him with an ultimatum that surprises him considering his many years of faithful service: drop all charges or receive a dishonorable discharge without pension for violating the company's code of conduct. Yellow chooses a third option—disclosing all of the company's overseas branch's acts of embezzlement and other forms of corruption to the media. Following this betrayal, Yellow escapes to an unnamed country with no extradition treaty and begins to work on a book that will reveal even further classified past operations.

Although Yellow, as a former intelligence officer, is thorough in guarding himself, eventually, it is Yellow himself that brings his own ruin upon him. Yellow's situation changes drastically after a coup d'état in his home country. The company proposes to Yellow that it will reinstate him if he reveals the previous regime's operations. Yellow accepts this offer and recites "the stories of counter-intelligence work, undercover work, false accusations,

배신할 수 있는 것이다. 그러나 조직에 해를 끼치기 위해 겨누었던 칼은 결국 자신의 목을 찌르고 만다. 정교하고 거대한 시스템을 향한 한 개인의 도전은 이처럼 무용하다.

자신의 이해에만 매달렸던 옐로와는 정반대편에 놓여 있는 정보원이 바로 브라운이다. 브라운은 해외 주재원으로 블랙이 처음 옐로를 처리하기 위해 공항에 도착했을 때부터 블랙을 돕는다. 브라운은 향수병과 스트레스에 시달리며, 처음 만난 블랙에게 "형님이라 불러도 되죠?"(26쪽)라고 말할 정도로 인간적인 구석이 있다. 브라운은 일을 믿는 블랙과는 달리 "저는 인간을 믿어서 그렇게 냉정하질 못하겠네요."(36쪽)라고 말하는 휴머니스트이다. 이 말을 남기고 사라진 브라운은 쿠데타로 혼란이 계속 되는 고국의 민병대 지도자가 되어 텔레비전에 나타난다. 그는 인간을 믿고, 자유의지를 믿은 결과 혼란의 와중에 가족을 잃고 민병대 지도자가 된 것이다.

마지막 정보기관원은 이 작품의 초점화자인 블랙이다. 옐로를 처리(암살 혹은 납치)하기 위해 파견된 블랙은, 옐로의 일거수 일투족을 감시한다. "뭘 믿느냐가 중

fabricated evidence, and cover-ups" that were all committed under the previous regime. As Black correctly concludes, this last action will invariably spell Yellow's own death. The previous regime has every reason to kill him. Those who assumed power by coup d'état also have no reason to try to prevent his death when they can blame it on the previous regime. Yellow, the master of destruction, an agent who destroyed "whatever organization had to be destroyed," invites his own destruction, blinded by his yearning to return home and his obsessive desire to restore his honor.

For Yellow, being an intelligence agent is simply his livelihood. The sense of the mission and loyalty are nothing more than ornaments to him. It is for this reason that he is able to betray an entire organization merely for the sake of his wounded pride. But the knife he aims at his former organization ends up slicing into his own neck. In this way Choi seems to suggest that an individual's challenge to a bureaucracy of this size and power is ultimately as futile as Yellow's actions.

On the opposite pole to Yellow's, there is the overseas agent Brown. Brown assists Black, who has come to handle Yellow's crisis, when he arrives at the airport. Brown suffers from acute homesick-

요한 게 아냐. 믿는 게 중요한 거지."(24쪽)라고 말하는 블랙이 믿는 것은 바로 자신의 "일"(26쪽)이다. 이처럼 블랙은 성찰이 결여된 도구적 이성의 극단적인 모습을 체화한 인물이다. 오직 그에게는 조직의 명령과 그것의 완벽한 수행만이 중요한 과제일 뿐이다.

그러나 조국의 쿠데타는 옐로와 브라운의 삶을 뒤집어 놓았듯이, 블랙의 삶 역시 그냥 내버려두지 않는다. 블랙은 어렵게 국장과 통화를 하지만, 국장은 "분명한 게 없어"(36쪽)라는 말을 남긴다. 그리고는 허둥지둥 "임무에는 변동사항이 없어. 목표를 시야에서 놓치지 말고 대기하도록 해."(38쪽)라는 말을 남기고, 전화는 곧 끊어진다. 국장에게는 그날 이후로 아무런 연락이 없다. 블랙은 "세상의 종말이란 모두가 죽어버리는 게 아니라 이런 식으로 홀로 잊히는 게 아닌가 하는 생각"(42쪽)을 한다. 블랙이 귀국을 준비할 무렵 국장이 아닌 사람에게서 전화가 걸려오지만, 블랙은 자신이 이전 정부와 현 정부 사이에 놓인 애매한 존재임을 다시 한 번 확인할 뿐이다. 그토록 조직과 일에만 헌신했던 블랙에게 남겨진 것은 완전한 버려짐이었던 것이다. 애당초 조직과 시스템에 블랙이란 개인의 자리는 없었던 것인지도

ness and stress. He is unabashedly human, asking Black when he meets him for the first time, "May I call you *hyeongnim*?" Unlike Black, who believes in his work, Brown is a humanist: "I believe in people, so I can't just stay calm." Brown disappears after saying this and resurfaces on a news broadcast as a militia commander. A believer in the people and free will, he has become a militia commander after the loss of his entire family.

The third agent, Black, is the narrative focus of this story. Dispatched to handle—assassinate or kidnap—Yellow, Black follows Yellow's every movement. At one point he offers his mantra to Brown to attempt to ease his accomplice's conscience: "What you believe in doesn't matter. It's the believing that matters." Black himself "believe[s] that this is [his] job." Black is the sort of agent who does not think, a person who embodies instrumental rationality. What matters to him is the order of his organization and his successful completion of that task.

However, the coup d'état in his country affects Black as well when it turns Yellow's and Brown's lives upside down. When Black finally manages to establish contact with his director, the director informs him with little else beyond, "Nothing's clear."

모른다.

블랙은 자신의 암살 대상(전 정부)이자 보호 대상(현 정
부)이기도 한 옐로의 오피스텔을 찾아간다. 블랙은 사
소한 대화를 나누며 입사 초기에 같은 팀에서 함께 일
한 적도 있는 옐로와 오붓한 시간을 즐기지만, 민병대
를 향한 옐로의 독설에 폭발하고 만다. 민병대의 부대
장인 브라운은 자신들이 가족을 잃었다며 절대로 복수
를 포기하지 않을 거라는 인터뷰를 한다. 그러한 인터
뷰 화면을 보며 옐로는 "살려둬서는 안 되지. 저런 새끼
들은 싹 쓸어버려야 돼."(68쪽)라고 말한다. 블랙은 "가
족을 잃은 사람들입니다."(68쪽)라고 말하지만, 그런 것
은 아무것도 아니라며 "돌아가면 저것들부터 처리할
거"(70쪽)라고 덧붙인다. 그 순간 블랙은 옐로를 죽인다.
이 순간 스스로 자유를 반납한 채 노예 되기를 선택했
던 블랙은 드디어 하나의 주체가 되기를 선택한 것이
다. 블랙은 그동안 하나의 온전한 주체가 아니었다. 그
에게는 어떤 사건이 현실의 인과관계로부터 전적으로
독립된 자기원인에서 비롯된 것인가를 묻는 형식으로
서의 자유가 존재하지 않았기 때문이다. 회사의 명령과
는 무관하게 옐로를 살해하는 이 순간, 블랙은 '그럼에

His last words truly cement Black's limbo-state in a foreign world: "There's no change in your mission. Don't lose your target and stand by." In lieu of this Black prepares to return home but he finally receives a call from someone other than his director. This call only confirms Black's impression that he remains in a gray area between former and current regimes. The only thing left for Black, who has dedicated his entire life to an organization and to his work, is to be completely abandoned by the system. There has probably never been a place for any individual in the organization and system anyway.

Eventually, Black does manage to finally visit Yellow, his previous assassination target and now current protected asset. Black enjoys small talk with him, reminiscing over their brief common work in past operations, but eventually reacts to Yellow's words regarding the militia. While watching Brown on television inform a TV interviewer that he has already lost his entire family and that he will never give up until he has his revenge, Yellow declares, "We shouldn't let them live! We should wipe out all those sons-of-bitches!" Black responds with, "They lost their families," but Yellow dismisses it and offers the cold promise, "I'm going to take care

도 자유로워라'라는 칸트식의 자유를 떠안은 것이다.

작품의 마지막에 블랙이 간부용 직통라인으로 하는 보고는 사실상 담당자가 아닌 자기 자신을 향한 것에 가깝다. 이때의 임무 완수는 모든 조직에서 벗어나 자기의 자유의지를 회복했다는, 그리하여 비로소 자신이 온전한 인간이 되었다는 보고에 다름 아니다. 그러나 이 한 건의 살인 행위로 블랙은 자유를 얻을 수 있을까? 당연히 세상과 시스템은 그처럼 간단하지 않다. 그것은 옐로의 죽음이, 브라운의 고투가 증명하는 바이다. 불꽃도, 연기도, 사이렌 소리도 나지 않는데 뒤를 돌아보는 블랙의 행위는 진정한 자유가 블랙에게도 결코 쉽지만은 않을 것임을 암시적으로 드러낸다.

이경재 서울대학교 국어국문학과 및 동 대학원을 졸업했고, 2006년 《문화일보》 신춘문예 평론부문에 당선되었다. 현재 숭실대학교 국어국문학과 교수로 재직하고 있다. 저서로 『단독성의 박물관』 『한설야와 이데올로기의 서사학』 『한국 현대소설의 환상과 욕망』 『끝에서 바라본 문학의 미래』 등이 있다.

of them first thing as soon as I return home." That very moment, Black kills Yellow. Black, who has given up his freedom and has instead chosen to be a slave, chooses to become his own agent at that moment. Prior to this, Black was not able to be his own agent; he lacked the basic freedom to make his own independent judgments completely free from the context of an outside reality. But at the very moment when Black murders Yellow, ignoring his company's orders, Black becomes the bearer of a kind of Kantian freedom.

At the very end, Black's report on the hot line is a report more for his own sake than for his former company. His accomplished mission here is to recover his own free will regardless of any organizational needs, allowing himself to become a whole human being again. But does Black really acquire freedom through this one act of murder? Naturally, the world and the system are not that simple. This is proven by Yellow's death and Brown's struggle. At the end of the story, Black turns around to have one last look at Yellow's former home. There are no flames, smoke, or sirens, but there is much to leave behind. In the end, perhaps true freedom still may not come easily for individuals like Black.

Lee Kyung-jae Lee studied Korean literature as an undergraduate and graduate student at Seoul National University. he made his literary debut in 2006 by winning the criticism award at *the Munhwa Ilbo* Spring Literary contest. Currently a professor of Korean literature at Sungsil University, he has published *Museum of Individuality*, *Han Solya and the Narratology of Ideology*, and *Illusion and Desire in Modern Korean Novel*, and *The Future of Literature Seen From the End*.

비평의 목소리
Critical Acclaim

무엇보다도 최민우 소설의 좋은 점은 이 세계를 바라보는 치열하면서도 건강한 시선이고 패기다. 심사 과정에서 그의 소설 문장이 다소 거친 듯하다는 지적이 있었지만 그런 흠조차 덮을 만큼 그의 소설에는 설명하기 어려운 어떤 감동이 있다. 그것은 아마도 어떤 식으로든 작가 자신을 둘러싼 현실을 감각하고 인지하는 작가 나름의 개성적인 문제의식 덕분일 것이다.

심진경, 「신인상 본심 심사평」, 《자음과 모음》 NO. 18,

자음과 모음, 2012.

또 한편 특별하게 본 신인의 작품은 최민우의 「이베

Above all, the virtue of Choi Min-woo's works is his keen, yet healthy perspective and aspiration towards reality. Although we thought his sentences were at times rough, there are inexplicably moving qualities in his works that compel us to overlook even those minor blemishes. This is probably because his unique insights into reality surround him in various ways.

Shim Jin-gyeong, "Judges' Remarks on Selecting Final New Writer's Awardee," *Jaeumgwa Moeum* 18 (2012)

Another new writer's work that stood out for us was "Dishonored" by Choi Min-woo. The narration of this story is so vivid and suspenseful that I could

리아의 전갈」이었다. 이 작품은 읽는 내내 영화와 같은 화면이 자꾸 머릿속에 그려질 만큼 활동적이고 매 장면마다 영화의 클라이맥스처럼 아슬아슬함을 느끼게 한다. 이야기가 반전에 반전을 거듭하며 끝까지 흥미롭게 진행된다. 입으로 읽고 귀로 전달받는 느낌으로도 이 작품의 강점이 잘 살아날 것 같다.

이순원, 「선정 경위 및 심사평」, 『제2회 EBS 라디오 문학상 작품집』,
김영사ON, 2014.

최민우는 예리한 작가이다. 그것은 한두 단어로 인물이나 상황의 리얼리티를 포착해내는 거의 본능과도 같은 감각에서 비롯되는 날카로움이다. 삼류 사회자가 구사하는 단어 하나, 인물이나 사물의 이름 하나, 소도구 하나를 통하여 최민우는 그 상황의 실감을 거의 완벽하게 포착하여 전달하는 능력을 지니고 있다.

이경재, 「평설」, 『2014 젊은 소설』, 문학나무, 2014.

see every scene in my head as if I were watching a movie. Choe's story continues to grab our attention until the very end through reversal after reversal. This work's merits are well registered through our various sensations.

Lee Sun-won, "*Judges*' Remarks on the Selection," The 2nd EBS Radio Literary Award Recipients Story Collection (Gimm-Young Publishers, 2014)

Choi Min-woo is a sharp writer. His sharpness, embodied in his ability to capture a person's or a circumstance's reality in nothing but a single word or two, seems almost instinctual. One can see this ability most clearly when Choi's captures a situation's reality perfectly using only a single word a third-rate MC might use, a name of a person or a thing, or a prop.

Lee Kyung-jae, "Critical Commentary," *The 2014 Young Stories* (Munhak Namu, 2014)

K-픽션 005
이베리아의 전갈

2014년 8월 29일 초판 1쇄 인쇄 | 2014년 9월 5일 초판 1쇄 발행

지은이 최민우 | 옮긴이 전승희 | 펴낸이 김재범
기획위원 정은경, 전성태, 이경재
편집 정수인, 이은혜, 윤단비, 김형욱 | 관리 박신영 | 디자인 이춘희
펴낸곳 (주)아시아 | 출판등록 2006년 1월 27일 제406-2006-000004호
주소 서울특별시 동작구 서달로 161-1(흑석동 100-16)
전화 02.821.5055 | 팩스 02.821.5057 | 홈페이지 www.bookasia.org
ISBN 979-11-5662-043-3(set) | 979-11-5662-048-8 (04810)
값은 뒤표지에 있습니다.

K-Fiction 005
Dishonored

Written by Choi Min-woo | **Translated by** Jeon Seung-hee
Published by Asia Publishers | 161-1, Seodal-ro, Dongjak-gu, Seoul, Korea
Homepage Address www.bookasia.org | **Tel**. (822).821.5055 | **Fax**. (822).821.5057
First published in Korea by Asia Publishers 2014
ISBN 979-11-5662-043-3(set) | 979-11-5662-048-8 (04810)

금기와 욕망 Taboo and Desire